RENATA
VITALI
USA TODAY BESTSELLING AUTHOR
parker s. huntington

MORE BOOKS

Asher Black
Niccolaio Andretti
Ranieri Andretti
Bastiano Romano
Renata Vitali
Damiano De Luca
Marco Camerino
Rafaello Rossi
Lucy Black

Damiano De Luca is a curse without a cure.

Before he ruled the De Luca family,
before he became the man everyone feared,
before he scoured an empire in search of me,
he chose me to ruin.

I was innocent.
An untainted princess.
The heiress to the Vitali mafia throne.

And I was in the wrong place at the wrong time
when I met the wrong boy.

My name is Renata Vitali,
and this is not a love story.

AUTHOR'S NOTE

Hey, readers!

It always intimidates me to write the author's note. It means that this—my dream, being an author—is real. It also means I'm about to send another book into the world—scared, excited, and a million other emotions I can't name.

I'll start with the easy stuff. This is a novella. It ends in a cliffhanger and is the prequel to *Damiano De Luca*. Fair warning!

This is the story of how Damian and Renata meet. It's also a story of learning how and *who* to trust—your friends, family… yourself. Sometimes, the people you should be able to trust are the last people you can. Sometimes, you find refuge in unexpected people, people you're scared to trust yet 100% should.

When you find yourself at a crossroads, looking at a path you're familiar with and an unknown path that makes your heart pound just thinking of it, trust yourself to make the right choice, to take a leap of faith, and to be happy.

In my author's notes, I love to talk about what I learned from each book and what I went through while writing and publishing it. Usually, I write a book and it ends up mirroring what I'm going through *as* I write it. However, this time, *after* I wrote Renata and Damian's story, I noticed the lessons I learned kept popping up in my life.

I'm the type of person who gives people a second chance. Then a third. A forth. And so on. Then, I thought of Damian and Renata's story and realized I don't owe anyone my trust. I don't have to give chance after chance. I can break free. I can choose better people to trust. People who really deserve it.

Don't be afraid to leave something or someone you know because you feel you need to stay, or you're comfortable staying, or you're afraid of change. Break the mold. Trust yourself. Choose yourself. The right people for you will be the ones who choose you back.

WITH SO, SO, SO MUCH LOVE,

Parker

camerino
romano
rossi
de luca
andretti
WA
OR
CA
NV
ID
MT
WY
UT
CO
AZ
NM
ND
SD
NE
KS
OK
TX
MN
IA
MO
AR
LA
WI
IL
MI
IN
KY
TN
MS
AL
GA
FL
SC
NC
VA
WV
PA
NY
VT
ME
NH
MA
CT
RI
NJ
DE
MD
DC

For Chloe.

I miss you.

Life hurts without you.

The devil doesn't come dressed in a red cape and pointy horns. He comes as everything you've ever wished for. Pray for wisdom and discernment.

— TUCKER MAX, ASSHOLES FINISH FIRST

Trust

trəst/

Noun

Firm belief in the reliability, truth, ability, or strength of someone or something.

Trust is a series of decisions. It's your choice to give it, and the people you give it to have the choice to prove you right. One day, the time will come when it's you you'll have to decide to trust. When that time comes, trust yourself. Then, let your heart prove you right.

PROLOGUE

> "Trusting you is my decision.
> Proving me right is your choice.
>
> — UNKNOWN

DAMIANO DE LUCA

They say, one day, it will hurt less. The distance will stop seizing my throat and let me breathe. It'll feel okay to wake up, pat the space beside me, and not feel her there. It'll be easier to tell a joke and realize the only person who can understand it isn't there to hear it. They say, one day, you'll find someone else, and you'll feel these same things for her.

They say these things, but not a night passes where she doesn't cross my mind.

She's either my curse or my angel.

RENATA VITALI

Damiano De Luca is the hardest challenge I've ever faced. He is my only leap of faith. My I-fell-fast, I-fell-hard, I-jumped-first-and-asked-later, and only-he-can-pick-me-back-up first love. He's my think of you every night. My wake up reaching for you. My never-be-the-same goodbye. My heart's biggest enemy.

And me? I am *his* first love.

But I don't want to be his first love. I want to be his last love.

The truth is, this story is not a love story.

ONE

> Love all, trust a few, do wrong to none.
>
> —WILLIAM SHAKESPEARE

RENATA VITALI

My fingers gripped the leather armrest as the plane skidded across the tarmac at Devil's Landing. I supposed most small Texas towns didn't have the luxury of a private airstrip, but Devils Ridge wasn't a typical small town.

With cute lighthouses scattered across its coastal edges, Devils Ridge would have been quaint and scenic—had there not been a cumbersome mafia presence. It was the second oldest city in Texas, with its first colonial settlement dating back to the 1700s. A couple of hundred years later, a new devil settled in Devils Ridge—Ludovico De Luca, the first De Luca to taint the town.

In the Vitali archives, there were books documenting Ludovico's descent into madness. After his son's wife had given birth, he slaughtered them both and raised his grandchild to be crazier than him. The De Lucas bred each generation with no moral code, and I was entering the lion's den.

I traced my fingers along the wood-trimmed table in front of me. My last name, Vitali, laid etched in the center, along with our centuries-old coat of arms. Laurel leaves. Lion. Torch. Purple. Peace. Courage. Intelligence. *Royalty*.

There were Italian mafia syndicates all over the world, but the major syndicates were the five American syndicates—Romano, Andretti, De Luca, Camerino, and Rossi. Hundreds of years ago, ruthless wars broke out across the globe. Syndicates fought other syndicates for territories and honor. Two syndicates in Europe wiped out. Thousands dead. Millions wasted. Only then did every syndicate agree to gather for peace talks in Italy.

My family—the Vitali—ran the peace talks. Since then, my family has governed the syndicates, making sure no syndicate crossed the line. The Vitali had our own armies. We had our own deep coffers. And we had our own hierarchy, where my father—*il condottiero*—was the boss who sat at the top, and I was the lone mafia princess.

It sounded glamorous, but in reality, it was a tyrannical father, an unconventional upbringing, and a life of boarding schools… and now, being shipped to De Luca territory as punishment.

"Miss Vitali?" Seven years ago, Ivo had been the flight attendant on my flight from Italy to my junior boarding school in Connecticut, and he'd stuck with me since. Which was how he knew what I wanted as my eyes shifted across his attire. "No phones, Ren. Your papà gave strict instructions."

I hated when he used my nickname. It drained my anger like watching Netflix with 3G drained my iPhone battery. "I didn't ask."

He *tsked* and gave me his arm, helping me to my feet until my five-six frame stood eye-level with his shoulder. My cheap, dyed-blonde hair rested in a samurai bun on the top of my head, and between my bare face and the sweats that covered my long legs, I gave the accurate impression that I didn't want to be here. I doubted I could find any rational syndicate member outside the De Luca family who'd want to be here.

Ivo led me down the stairs and off the plane. "Your things will arrive at the De Luca manor later tonight." He eyed the town car resting a few feet from the base of the stairs. Tinted windows. Dark and shiny. Vanity plates, whereas most mafiosos preferred unmarked and nondescript. "Are you sure you're okay?"

What did he want me to do? Blink twice if I needed saving? I nodded my head but blinked twice anyway. You never knew when someone would surprise you.

Displays of affection were as rare to me as beluga sturgeon caviar, but I leaned forward and wrapped my twig-like arms around Ivo's neck anyway. "I'll miss you, Ivo. You be good now, alright?"

And I would. Since I was nine, Ivo had shuffled me the thirty-minute flight from boarding school to Maman every weekend. I'd seen him far more than I'd seen my own father, and now I didn't know when I would see him again.

"I should be telling you that, Miss Vitali. I trust there will be no trouble from you, little one." He kissed my forehead and waited until the driver opened the car door to leave.

Don't look back. Don't look back. Don't look back.

I looked back, and a tear slipped past my lashes as the plane door closed behind Ivo. I pretended to sneeze into my hand, so I could wipe away the tear without anyone noticing. But when I entered the Rolls Royce, came face to face with Devils Ridge's Head Devil, and was gifted a knowing sneer, I knew I fooled no one.

Angelo De Luca out-dressed me in his three-piece bespoke suit, his hair slicked back and his manicured nails gripping an oversized cigar. "Well, well, well. Pleasure to meet you, Miss Vitali." His leery eyes lined my skin with goosebumps as I settled into the back seat, thankful for the middle console separating us. Neither of us spoke as his ogling continued. "So, Daddy sent his bad little girl here for punishment, huh?"

No, Daddy got caught eating between his secretary's legs for lunch and sent his daughter to Middle of Nowhere, Texas before she could tell his wife. It wasn't my fault my father couldn't keep his dick clean the one week I surprised him with a visit. I wondered who Angelo would think was the bad guy in that scenario. Probably me.

I didn't respond, instead reaching for the tablet attached to the back of the seat in front of me. Angelo's hand gripped my wrist tightly, proving just how much of a farce his name was. There wasn't a trace of angel in this man.

I yanked my hand away and forced myself not to cradle the bruised flesh with my other hand. Dad's phone ban would be a nuisance, but it wouldn't stop me from finding one and spilling what I'd seen to Maman. I didn't want to be here. I doubted I could find any rational syndicate member outside the De Luca family who'd want to be here.

I didn't know why he even bothered keeping up the pretense of their marriage. They didn't live in the same country. It's not like they fooled anyone, let alone one another. Dad lived in Italy, where I visited him once a year, and Maman lived a short thirty-minute flight from my Connecticut boarding school, where I visited her every weekend.

We passed a strip club parallel to the airport's landing strip, and the words "The Landing Strip" glowed from the neon sign.

"My club." Angelo eyed my chest beneath the baggy weight of my oversized Blink 182 tee. "You're welcome to visit if you'd like. I'm sure you would fit right in, darlin'."

I ignored him, looking out the window as the driver cruised past rows of large Victorian-style homes. It seemed like time had touched nothing in Devils Ridge, and had it not been for the very twenty-first-century car we rode in, I'd have thought someone trapped us in the mid-1800s.

After the car passed a double set of looming iron gates and made its way down a tree-canopied driveway, Angelo passed something black, plastic, and rectangular to me.

I took it from his outstretched fingers, taking painstaking care not to touch him. "What's this?"

"A pager." A sneer curved his thin lips. "Signore Vitali said you're to have no contact with a phone, and I'll need a way to contact you."

I pocketed the thing, amusement consuming me as he eyed my sweats with a curled upper lip. *Only a fool looks at strength and sees weakness.* Maman had first told me this when I missed the growth spurt all of my peers seemed to share at the same time. She was right.

By middle school, I reached my growth spurt and boasted cascading brown hair with natural waves, which bounced like Victoria's Secret models' when they strut down runways. My eyes boasted a shade of amber I liked to call evil, but Maman always referred to as rapturous. And eighth-grade boys referred to the slight Italian accent which adorned my voice as "exotic."

I hated the attention. Hated the way it made girls scowl and boys stare. Hated the way my teachers thought differently of me. Hated the expectations that came with looking and sounding like I did.

As soon as Maman let me, I started dying my hair a simple blonde, adopted a flawless General American accent, and found a pair of mousy, prescription-free glasses I occasionally wore. When I left junior boarding school and entered boarding school, I no longer had to build pretend friendships. People overlooked me, just like I had intended.

And now, sitting beside the head of the De Luca family, I knew he overlooked me, too. Angelo's leery gazes and rough touch were an intimidation tool. But in doing so, he'd laid his cards out for me to see. He thought I was weak. Too weak to earn anything more than brute intimidation tactics when subtlety would have worked better.

He was a fool, and I didn't need other people to validate my strength. I'd get through this exile with my head on my shoulders by being overlooked and savvy. There was no other way.

The driver opened the door, shooting a gust of hot Texas wind at me. I took his offered hand, righted myself, and stepped as far away from Angelo as I could without being too obvious. I followed Angelo up a set of stone stairs to a giant Victorian manor that had probably been built somewhere around 1850, like most of the houses in Devils Ridge.

The white trim stood out amongst the near-black stones. When I entered through the double doors two butlers held open, I saw that the dark wood floors matched the gloomy exterior. The house looked cold, like despite its age, it hadn't been lived in.

Angelo led me past a spiral staircase and into a hallway. He opened the second to last door but stayed at the doorway. "This is your room." He stepped to the door across from my new room and opened it. It led to an honest-to-God bathing pool, like the ones in public bathhouses. "This is the East wing bathroom. The house is pre-Victorian, and the plumbing reflects it. While it's been renovated twice, once to reflect late Victorian-era homes of the time and more recently to introduce modern amenities, we couldn't add more bathrooms without altering the historical integrity of the home." He nearly growled at his own words.

Right. Because I was supposed to believe Angelo De Luca cared about 'historical integrity.' We stepped out of the bathroom, and he closed the door. I waited for him to say something else.

Instead, he leaned a hip against a wall, crossed his arms, and stared me down. "I don't want you here. I don't like your family thinking they run the five syndicates." We *did* run the five syndicates. At least, it was our duty to police them. "And I certainly don't like the idea of you spying on us. There's nothing to see here. Nothing to report."

I considered my options. I could lower my head and act meek. That was usually my go to, but I doubted it was the best option here. If I pushed over, Angelo would continue to stomp over me, and he didn't seem to have that filter in him that made good decisions—like not laying a hand on me.

So, I tilted my head and chilled him with a condescending smirk. "That's not why I'm here." My strong, level voice held no inflection. "Remember your place, De Luca. Behind the Vitali. Behind the Romano. Behind the Andretti. Behind the Rossi. Behind the Camerino. What's it like to stand firmly at the end of the five syndicates?"

He raised his finger and waved it at me. "Now you watch your mouth, you little slut."

I looked down at my attire, my body language clearly uninterested and unfazed. "I don't think slut means what you think it means, Angelo."

He opened his mouth to speak, thought better of it, and closed it. When he opened it again, he was no less calm, but he had a satisfied smile on his face as he seethed, "You'll share the bathroom with my son, Damiano, whose room is beside yours."

Wait.

Angelo De Luca had a son?!

TWO

> "Whether it's a friendship or relationship, all bonds are built on trust. Without it, you have nothing.
>
> — UNKNOWN

DAMIANO DE LUCA

Like any sane person, I spent as little time as possible in Angelo's mansion. It used to feel like mine, too, back when Mama was still alive. Nowadays, I spent more time at the local strip club than I did in my childhood home. Not that strippers were my thing. Networking with the people who worked there and those who enjoyed their services, however, was my thing.

Miriam stood in front of me, clad in cheap lingerie and too many bruises to count. I eyed them, cataloging each and every one of them before meeting her eyes. "He's hitting you again, Mir."

Miriam had become my dad's consiglieri's mistress around the same time my balls dropped. Angelo's advisor beat his wife, so the eggplant-colored bruises lining Mir's tanned skin didn't surprise me. Expecting this didn't mean I accepted it. It pissed me the fuck off, but one day, I'd be in charge of the De Luca syndicate, and these problems wouldn't exist.

"Don't worry your handsome face about me, Damian. I'll be fine." She normally never spoke this freely, but the private room in The Landing Strip gave us some protection from Angelo's goons, which I'd hoped would open her up.

"Why'd he hit you?"

Her head lowered, another punch to my gut. Battered women reminded me of my mother—and every time I stood by and watched her get trampled by my father and come back begging for more. Helpless to stop it.

I stepped forward, placed two fingers beneath Mir's chin, and tilted her head up as gently as I could. In her glassy powder blue eyes, I examined my reflection. Neat gentleman's cut. Dark eyes. Aquiline nose. Sharp classic Italian features. A hint of stubble I'd shave tomorrow.

My muscular six-two frame towered over her, too, so I worked to soften my expression as I spoke to her. "You can trust me, Mir. I'll protect you."

"Your father—"

"My father is a dinosaur. Have you seen the arms on a T-Rex? They can't reach far. He can't touch you, Mir. I won't let him."

She smiled and breathed out a short laugh. "You'd make a great boss for the De Luca syndicate, Damiano."

That was the plan.

She shook her head, and fear widened her eyes. "I shouldn't have said that." She looked around. "I-I didn't mean that. It's so easy to forget what to say when you're so nice." Her eyes closed before opening again. "Angelo De Luca is a wonderful boss. You won't tell yyour dad I implied otherwise, r-right?"

"Mir, I'm not my father. You don't need to watch your words. You don't need to be scared. I don't like seeing bruises on your skin. I don't like the way your hands shake when you speak to me. None of this is right. Do you understand that?"

She nodded her head. "I don't know what to do, Damian. I can't run away. My whole family lives here. I can't leave them!" Her father was a low ranking De Luca, but a loyal one who'd never leave De Luca territory. "I can't do anything."

Pressing her would do neither of us any good. So, I nodded my head and put a comfortable amount of distance between us. "If you need anything, you can come to me, Miriam."

"Thank you. You've been a good friend."

That was the point. Don't get me wrong. I genuinely cared for Miriam, and her safety genuinely concerned me… but despite being low ranking, Mir's dad had a wide network of friends in the De Luca syndicate. He'd be the perfect ally to help me dethrone my father.

Miriam patted my cheek and left. I stayed a few minutes in the room, ruffled my hair so it looked like I'd fallen out of bed, and scrunched my plain t-shirt in a few places to form wrinkles. One task down. Another to go.

Reaching into my pocket, I pulled out a Gurkha Black Dragon cigar, unrolled it, and pulled out the sheet of paper hidden in it. A twelve-hundred-dollar cigar ruined. Just like that. An unknown benefactor had been sending me cigars with hidden messages in them for the past year. Did I like being uninformed? Hell, no. But I wasn't in the position to deny help.

This time, I read the message, my feelings more mixed than normal. Befriending Miriam to use her later felt dirty. Necessary, but dirty. Would it have felt less dirty if it hadn't been a suggestion from The Benefactor? Probably. Either way, I couldn't change these things, so I focused on my next task.

Unseat the *consiglieri*.

I rolled my eyes. Not as easy as it sounded, but hell, I'd try. Anything to get my dad off that throne and away from my people. People who deserved better than the best Angelo could give them, especially since he gave them the worst.

The keys to my matte black Range Rover clanged in my pockets as I left The Landing Strip, nodding my goodbyes to everyone as I walked out. Most of the De Luca members gathered here in between work, which made it the best place to network. Baby steps in my master plan.

By the time I reached my hallway, Angelo had left for dinner, just like I knew he would. Seeing him as little as possible helped maintain my sanity. Araceli walked down the hall with a pile of sheets in her hands, which was odd given the hour. The housekeeping staffed usually retired to their quarters by now.

I thought she'd step by me, but instead, she smiled, dipped her head in a polite bow, and eyed my body like she'd been doing for quite some time now. I arched a brow. "Yes?"

Her face flushed, and she looked around—probably searching for something sensible to say—before her eyes returned to mine, and she whispered, "Have you met the Vitali girl? I've never met a Vitali before. She's kind of… frumpy?"

I paused at her words, my eyes narrowed and head tilted. "Vitali girl?" I racked my brain for any gossip of her I could remember, surprised by how easily it came to me.

Renata Vitali. Sixteen. Only child. Daughter of Margot Vitali and the head of the Vitali. Supposedly smart.

Araceli's frown creased the skin between her brows, and she dropped the flirting. "You didn't know she was coming?"

No, I hadn't.

A powerful unknown entity had entered my territory, and I didn't know. My jaw ticked. It was just like Dad to keep something like this from me. I wanted to brush it off. I wanted to push this information aside and focus on dethroning my father… but something in my gut told me this changed everything.

THREE

> Trust is earned when actions meet words.
>
> — CHRIS BUTLER

RENATA VITALI

Sometimes, you know when catastrophe is about to strike you. A screech of tires. Oxygen masks shooting at you from above your airplane seat. The numbness spreading across your face before a stroke.

There were no warning signs for me.

My heart was calm when Angelo De Luca turned the corner of the East Wing hallway, seconds after showing me what would be my room for however long Papà's punishment for me lasted.

My heart was calm when, not a minute later, I darted to the room next to mine, and my fingers twisted the door handle without a moment's hesitation.

My heart was calm as I eased my way into the bedroom. The one that belonged to the secret De Luca son. *Damiano,* his dad had called him, not an ounce of affection in his voice.

I should have known better.

In this world, there was only one reason to hide a child if you were a mafia boss for one of the Five Syndicates. The thought of learning firsthand what was wrong with Angelo De Luca's secret son should have scared me.

But in the rare moments I'd seen my father, he had taught me that fear was weakness, and weakness was death. It wasn't a quaint lesson, nor was it a father's honorable attempt at keeping his daughter safe.

It was a warning.

Against him.

He was the threat in my life. Always would be. I'd been here less than an hour, but every second I spent in Devils Ridge, Texas reminded me of that.

Don't be weak.

You're a Vitali.

Vitalis don't feel fear.

Christ, a whole continent away, and Papà's voice still plagued my mind. Usually, he inspired anger. Today, determination darted from my head to my toes as I began my search for a cell phone or landline in Damiano De Luca's room.

Like my room next door, this room felt un-lived in. Unlike my room, someone had been living in this one for longer than all of one point two seconds.

Telltale signs of neglect painted the room. Crisp, clean sheets—untouched for who knew how long. Aged air—stale with a fading hint of aftershave. A sole eighteenth-century dresser, coated with a fine layer of dust.

I should have considered what that meant. That even the maids hadn't entered this room in some time. I didn't. Maman deserved to know that I'd seen Papà pounding into his secretary before he sent me to Texas to live with the De Lucas—without a phone and beleaguered by explicit instructions never to be in contact with one, lest I be given an opportunity to tattle to Maman.

I wasn't the type to listen, but people were like scampering rats when it came to my family. Or maybe they were cult followers—frail and obeisant, followers begging for a command, all too happy to hide the electronics from me. This meant searching for a damn phone in foreign territory proved nearly impossible.

It startled me how much control Papà had over people, even an ocean away. As the head of the Vitali family, Papà was *il condottiero.* The leader. In layman's terms, if the syndicate territories across the world were states and their bosses were governors, the Vitali family would be the federal government. And Papà? He'd be president.

Still, he may have made the rules for the mafia underworld, but I made my own rules. Those included doing all I could to defy his. Like finding a phone. I scoured the room, optically tracing every inch.

My heart was calm as failure met my eyes. There was a neat stack of laundry on the desk, a journal that peeked out from beneath the pillow-top mattress, and a box with north of twenty-three grand worth of Gurkha Black Dragon cigars tucked away in a built-in humidor beside the Alaskan king-sized bed. But no phone.

Murmurs sounded from the hallway, and still, my heart was calm as I searched the room for a hiding place. Locked closet. Bathroom across the hall. Curtains tied so tightly together, even my thin waist couldn't hide behind them. Four-poster bed with a bottom blocked off by 18th century wood.

Silly, naive Renata Vitali.

Would I ever learn to plan for the worst?

Yet, my heart was calm when the handle to the bedroom door twisted, and I realized there was nowhere to hide.

My heart was calm as I perched myself in the center of the bed, looking as ready for my first encounter with Damiano De Luca as I could in old designer sweats stitched for rebellion and a samurai bun that weathered the eight-hour private flight from Italy to Texas.

My heart was calm as I accepted the inevitability of discovery with grace.

My heart was calm.

My heart was calm.

My heart was calm.

Until I saw him for the first time, and it wasn't.

FOUR

> "Trust is like an eraser.
> It gets smaller and smaller after every mistake.
>
> — UNKNOWN

DAMIANO DE LUCA

I prepared myself to meet the Vitali girl, but I didn't prepare to meet her in *my* room. My eyes landed on hers the instant I swung the door open. Surprise journeyed through my body, but I tampered it and studied her laying on my bed.

Shock flexed her fingers and widened her eyes, which told me all I needed to know. She'd never seen me before. Never even heard of me. This was confirmation that I was the De Luca syndicate's best kept secret. If a Vitali hadn't heard of me, no one had.

Renata's lips parted, and the urge to slip my thumb between them and stroke her tongue had my fingers itching. *This*. This reaction to her was the opposite of what I needed. Not now, when everything in my plan was starting to come together.

This made no sense. Her dark roots stained the edges of her shitty blonde dye job, she wore designer sweats like she starred in one of those rich housewives shows, and she'd piled her hair up in a lopsided ball on top of her head.

Still, her beauty stunned me. The type of beauty that attracted the worst attention. The kind that saw this girl and thought nothing but the dirty things he wanted to do to her. And I could see why. She was suggestive. Risqué. Lips so full they were the first thing you saw. Demure eyes you wanted to taint. Skin so milky you wondered how red it'd look after you bit down on it.

With her head cocked to the side, her eyes crawled down my body, like she was trying to figure me out. Probably trying to decide why she'd never heard of me. My father didn't want other syndicates to think there was a better alternative to him, and I didn't want to draw attention before I seized power.

Yet, as Renata gawked at me, trying her damnedest to hide it, I knew I caught her attention. She looked her age—sixteen on the brink of seventeen. But normal sixteen-year-old girls didn't stare at me like that. They stared at me with fear and lust, like they stared at a seven-figure handbag on the arm of today's hottest starlet. Unattainable. Worth more than they'd ever see in their lifetime.

But *her*. She stared at me like I was a reflection, and she was a looking glass. Her eyes—a goldish-red color impossible to define—tangled with mine. They fought. She won. It took three seconds too long to rebuild my barriers, but I knew she'd already seen the toll this life had taken on me.

Hardened edges. Tired lines. Haunted depths. She bore witness to it all, and it was too much to expect me to be nice after I'd caught her snooping in my room and she'd caught too many secrets in my eyes.

I hardened my features and took her in, taking painstaking care to eviscerate her with my intrusive glare. The frumpy attire—a distraction. The shitty dye job. The un-plucked brows. The chipped nail polish on bitten nails. The giant holes in her Converse.

Distraction. Distraction. Distraction.

Lies. Lies. Lies.

My lips formed a sneer, and I eyed where her body pressed against my bed. "If you want to sleep with me, you'll have to try harder, Princess."

Not because she didn't attract me. She did. More than anyone else I'd ever met. But because I'd have to be stupid to involve myself with a Vitali; she'd snooped in my goddamned room, where I concealed all my messages from The Benefactor; and the way she hid behind her clothes screamed liar, and I didn't fuck liars. Hell, if my dick touched a liar, it'd probably confuse her for my own hand.

Her flash of anger speared me, but she reined it in. The urge to whisper, *let loose, Princess. Fight me, beautiful,* gripped my throat until I swallowed. Twice. My throat bobbed violently both times, my mouth drier than I remembered it being ten minutes ago. Her anger intrigued me, urged me to dive in, unravel her secrets one by one until they became mine, and I knew all of her.

I wasn't a tyrant. I didn't need to know everything about everyone in my territory. Or maybe I'd just never been confronted by someone in Devils Ridge that I didn't know. Either way, I found myself in a peculiar position—off balance, too interested for my own damned good, and a little pissed off because of it.

Renata rose off the bed, her movements as graceful as her mafia royalty pedigree suggested. "Just seeing what I'm dealing with here."

My eyes tracked her body, tracing a path down the curves her baggy clothes hid until they returned to those amber orbs. She stared at me, her hand suspended in the air like she wanted to touch me. I cocked a brow, daring her to go for it, wondering what I'd do if she listened.

She took a small step backward, but I noticed it. My reflexes had my lips tilting upward, but I fought the urge to smile. This girl had fight. She had spine, and back bone, and all the things I never knew I wanted in her.

"Have your fill yet? I may have to charge admission, and I guarantee you can't afford the price." My tone spoke of the boredom I didn't feel.

She tilted her head up to meet my eyes. She was tall for her age, but I towered over her. "The most I'd part with for you is the gum beneath my shoe."

I wanted to laugh. She probably packed gum beneath her shoe just to keep people away.

My eyes slid down her body once again, focused on those holey Chucks, and returned to her face, expressionless given how much I riled her up—and I knew I riled her up. "I have no doubt you're the type with plenty of gum beneath your shoe."

Her brows furrowed together before she relaxed and straightened her shoulders. "Well, this has been riveting,"—indeed, it had—"but I'm jet lagged. Bye." She stepped forward before I could answer and bumped into my shoulder on her way out. A feisty princess, if I ever saw one.

It wasn't till my eyes scanned the room for signs of foul play, I counted and recounted my cigars, my fingers traced the cigar seams for any tears, and I decided nothing looked out of place that I realized she'd stolen my phone.

The princess was a little thief.

FIVE

> "I'm not upset that you lied to me,
> I'm upset that from now on I can't believe you.
>
> — FRIEDRICH NIETZSCHE

RENATA VITALI

The workers in the De Luca household liked to gossip in Spanish, which was close enough to my native Italian that I had an idea of what they said. Señor Damian, as the maids called him, came home more often than usual lately, and they blamed me.

I loathed the sense I saw in their logic.

If ever there was a cold war between two strangers, this was it. I'd stolen Damiano De Luca's phone. That didn't exactly set a remarkable first impression. He hadn't confronted me about it, but I knew he knew.

After sending Maman an email and erasing my digital tracks, I slipped the phone on the floor by his bedroom door. Maybe he would think he had dropped it.

A girl could hope.

That had been three days ago. Days passed, and tense silence thickened each time I heard him walk by my door. Thing was, I knew the heavy footsteps held intent. Syndicate royalty didn't make noise as they walked. Training took care of that.

But each firm step Damiano De Luca took was deliberate. Like a move made on a chessboard, thought ten steps ahead. In fact, life in the De Luca household felt exactly like a chess match, in which I held no control over the board.

Maman always had the Vienna match laid on the chessboard in her library. Every now and then, she'd move a piece. Sometimes, a week apart; sometimes, a year apart. The dark king never sees his demise coming, she'd tell me each time I noticed a moved piece.

But I'd spent enough time looking at that chessboard to see my demise coming. Heard the breaths of impending doom each time I left the confines of my room. Felt the ironclad fingers of vengeance wrap around my neck whenever I dared to sneak food from the kitchen. Smelled the metallic blood of ruin trickle down my body whenever I dodged across the hall to use the bathroom.

I sensed it now as I grabbed a change of clothes and darted to the bathroom I shared with Damian. Like the other houses in Devils Ridge, Texas, the De Luca household was antiquated. Built in the 18th century, the house had been renovated only twice—once during the Victorian era, so it matched the aesthetics of the other Victorian-style homes in town, and once again a few years ago when the contractors had decided that introducing anything more than the minimal number of modern amenities would jeopardize the historic integrity of the home.

Historic integrity, my ass.

The East Wing bathroom had three rooms—a toilet room, a vanity room, and a bathing room. The door to the bathroom led to the bathing room, where a small bathing pool laid in the center, like I was on the set of Game of Thrones.

It occurred to me what a waste of water filling and draining this pool was, but I wasn't going to bathe in Damian's soiled water. I slid my silk robe off my shoulders and hung it on the hook beside the door, along with my change of clothes.

One of the maids had warmed the pool and filled it with bubbles earlier, and I dipped a toe into the water, exploring the temperature. My waist barely kissed the water before the door swung open.

I moved quickly, covering my breasts with the bubbles as I plunged fully into the pool. My eyes met Angelo De Luca's as he stepped past the threshold, busting every myth about evil being incapable of entering a room uninvited. Or was that vampires?

"Miss Vitali." He took a step closer, and I forced myself not to move away from my spot against the closest pool edge to the door. How someone so slimy and decrepit could spawn someone who looked like Damiano De Luca was beyond me. "My sources tell me you turn seventeen years old today." The gap between us lessened. "Another year closer."

Another year closer to what?

Goosebumps traveled across my skin, and I forced myself not to eye the open door. It was late. The last of the East Wing staff had retreated to their quarters after drawing my bath. I trusted Angelo De Luca like I trusted a jock to do his own homework. I was alone with this sinister excuse of a man, and though calm had nestled itself inside my body from a young age, it burrowed deeper, hiding somewhere between apprehension and concern.

Still, I didn't allow my anxiety to manifest. I ignored him, reached for the shampoo, and formed a lather in my hair. A gust of wind flew in from the open door, chilling the exposed skin on my neck. I wanted to dip lower into the water, but being vulnerable in front of a man who enjoyed feasting on prey wasn't an option. Instead, I continued washing my hair.

His jaw ticked as I ignored him. "You are a guest in my household, Miss Vitali. You will not disrespect me."

"You're right." I tapped my foot beneath the water, hoping to expend the energy of my anxiety and replace it with amusement. "A person's a person, no matter how small."

Pretty sure that wasn't what Dr. Seuss had meant when he wrote that.

Oh, well.

Hard eyes burned my skin as some of the bubbles covering my breasts fizzled and died. "Careful, little girl." He crouched and reached out. I forced myself to act aloof as he cupped the side of my face and shut his teeth with an audible *snap!* "I bite."

During my boarding school's unit on Irish literature, I'd come across a Laurence Sterne quote: "Respect for ourselves guides our morals; respect for others guides our manners." Clearly, Angelo De Luca had neither, but it dawned on me that if I stayed here long, perhaps that would be my fate, too. I begged any higher power to not let me succumb to the De Luca madness.

Angelo's palm wandered down my cheek, past my collarbone, and toward my left breast. Goosebumps met his touch, and he cackled near my ear. "I scare you, don't I?"

He did, in the same way I feared poisonous spiders and walking home alone late at night. Logically. Clinically. And entirely detached. These things could hurt me if I let them, but I wouldn't let them.

"While we're exchanging fears, yours is my family." I stepped into his touch, enjoying the way his eyes flared in surprise. "I may fear you, Angelo, but I'll still face you. The fears we don't confront grow into limits, and I have no limits. But you?" I taunted him with my laughter. For a split second, I felt less like Harry Potter and more like Draco Malfoy. "You're bound by them each time you move."

"I could kill you right now, and we'd see just how scared I am of your family." Angelo's grip on my flesh became brutal, and his hand rested beneath the water, just short of reaching the top of my breast. Figured that'd be the time Damiano De Luca chose to enter the bathroom we shared.

His eyes took us in, narrowing on his dad's hand beneath the water for a split second before a sneer twisted his lips. "I put up with you fucking the help, Angelo," he spoke as if he owned the household, "but I will not put up with you further threatening the De Luca name by fucking the Vitali child."

The Vitali child.

Good grief. I'd asked the housekeepers for Damian's age. As of today, we were the same age, yet that was what I was to him. A child. Somehow, those words were all I could focus on. It wasn't lost on me that he may very well have just saved me from his father, but something I would come to learn about Damiano De Luca was that his presence crippled my logic. It didn't just cripple it. It nuked it, then buried it six feet under until I wasn't sure my logic had ever existed.

Angelo stood from his crouch, and I'd never seen so much hate a father held for his son as I saw in Angelo's eyes. "Finally home, son?"

Damian leaned a shoulder against the doorframe, amusement radiating off of him in waves, but I saw past the show he put on for his father. He was taunting him, just like I had taunted Angelo earlier. A defense tactic that shouldn't have built a connection between us—especially given the way he spoke of me as a child instead of an equal—but it did. "Obviously, if you're looking at me and we're in this house..."

Angelo met his son in three long strides until they stood mere inches apart. "One day, I will learn what it is that you do when you are gone, and I will destroy you."

A smarter man would have tempered his anger and hid his weaknesses. Instead, Angelo had laid his cards bare for me. The friction between him and his son and the ensuing power struggle between them weren't for outsider eyes and ears, but here I was, an unwilling voyeur with a front row seat. Who could blame me for pocketing the information?

Damian remained unfazed. "How can you destroy me when all you're capable of is self-destruction?"

And that was when I knew he would win. That he would *always* win. Calm, cool, and collected, Damiano De Luca was everything his father should have been as the head of one of the five American syndicates.

Damian's eyes shifted to me, reminding his father of the audience. Angelo pulled his shoulders back, standing taller than anyone in the room thought he was, and left.

My eyes met Damian's, and I wore the calmest expression I could manage. "Those who plot the destruction of others often perish in the attempt." I dipped my hair back into the water, rinsing the shampoo from my scalp. The tops of my breasts peeked out of the water at the movement, and I was painfully aware of my audience of one.

"Quoting Thomas Moore doesn't make you smart." His gaze swallowed mine as I lifted my head from the water, shock at his knowledge of the Irish poet driving my actions. "It makes you unoriginal."

"Coming from the boy plotting to dethrone his father, I'm not so sure I trust your judgment on originality. Read too many Marvel comics?" I grabbed the soap bar and ran it across my skin. "Is it the Loki and Odin relationship or the Blade and Lucas Cross relationship that inspires your every move?" My words may have lashed, but as I dipped the bar of soap under the water and rubbed at my body, I couldn't shake the feeling that I'd never been this physically vulnerable in front of another human.

But Damian wasn't his dad, and he didn't seem the slightest bit interested in my body. "You should have stayed out of things that are none of your business, Princess."

Excuse me?!

Being in Devils Ridge hadn't been a choice and being in this home had been even less of one. His father was the one who barged into the bathroom, and now Damian had the gall to accuse *me* of imposing? So much for kindred spirits.

If I were the type to lash out, I would have. Instead, I remained composed as I rinsed the rest of the soap from my shoulders, ascended the steps out of the pool, and stood in front of him. "If your intent is to provoke me, it's not working."

Water dripped from my naked flesh, but his eyes never wavered from mine. "I have no intent when it comes to you. You are a pest. A flea. Nothing more than a common house fly. Something that is beneath me to swat at. The door will remain open, and you'll eventually fly away. But until then, stay away from me and stay out of my business." Condescension was an ugly look on anyone but him. He stepped closer. "I wouldn't want to accidentally hurt you, Princess."

The air chilled my wet skin as it brushed against me. Or maybe it was his words that chilled me. That lasted for about a second before his father's voice boomed in the background as he yelled at one of the poor staff members in the opposite wing of the house.

Myriad emotions ran through Damian's eyes before he filtered them out. It didn't matter, though. The damage had been done. I'd seen the emotions, and rather than latching onto the moment of vulnerability like a vulture clutching onto a dead carcass, I saw a kindred spirit I wanted to help.

A damsel that needed saving.

I lifted my chin and measured my words. "I'm no princess."

He laughed at me. "What else would you be?"

I thought of Maman's chessboard and the never-ending Vienna game. I wasn't the king, but I certainly wasn't the pawn either. "I'd be the knight."

"Fine, Knight."

"Fine, Day."

His eyes narrowed at the nickname. I didn't wait for him to call me out on it as I reached for my robe, slipped it over my shoulders, and walked past him as collected as I could with a thin silk robe sticking to my wet skin.

Truth was, Day wasn't short for Damiano.

It was a play on Damsel.

He didn't know it yet, but that was exactly how I saw him.

It should have been a bad thing, but it wasn't.

The world might not have seen him as one, but to me, Damiano De Luca was the damsel— trapped in this gilded tower, lashing out at his dad for an escape—and I was the stupid knight in shining armor who wanted to save him.

> All the world is made of faith, and trust, and pixie dust.
>
> — J.M. BARRIE, *PETER PAN*

DAMIANO DE LUCA

Three months later

My favorite room in Angelo's mansion was the one he never stepped foot in. The library had been my sanctuary since I learned to read at age three. Mama took me in here, introduced me to a world of words that felt more real than my own, and filled it with thousands of books. When she died, this room was all I had left of her. A coffin of worn spines, first editions, and Dalbergia wood shelves.

So, it should have bothered me that Renata tainted my sanctuary each night when she crawled out of bed at two in the morning, crept inside here, and read the books that had previously only been touched by myself and my mother. But it didn't bother me. And that was dangerous.

For most of the summer, Renata locked herself in her room by day, the staff dropped food off to her room, and the only reprieve she had in this prison happened to be my reprieve, too. I understood that in ways I'd never tell anyone. It was why I left her to enjoy the library. Except today, when the lashing Angelo's belt had given me earlier still burned my back and the idea of company enticed me. Sue me.

Tonight, she was quiet as she crept out of her room. Not a single step heard. I stared at the framed article on Great-great-grandfather Ludovico De Luca as I waited for her to pass the painting of Ludo in the hall. (Angelo had an obsession with him.)

She pushed the double doors open, not a hint of surprise on her face when she saw me, though I know I surprised her. She was good at hiding. I'd give her that. But not from me. Never from me.

With my legs propped on two accent pillows formerly owned by a European prince three centuries ago, I laid on one of two ebony velvet divans in the library. A first edition copy of Fyodor Dostoevsky's *The Brothers Karamazov* rested between my palms. The same copy she'd been reading and left lying on the side table last night. I could still smell her vanilla scent on the cream pages.

She stood there for a moment, and I wondered how flustered I had her. I also wondered how smart she was. My contacts had informed me that she had the best education money could buy, and lust tempted me to test her.

"There are goosebumps rising along the length of your arms." I didn't once look up from the book. Even if I had, several feet separated us. I couldn't actually see the goosebumps, though I had no doubt they existed.

"I don't recall reading that line in the book." She sat on the divan across from mine, probably deciding this was better than another minute in her room.

I turned the page, not looking up, and continued with my test. "They're a physical manifestation of your attraction to me." My tone left little for debate. Like my words were fact—they were—and trying to argue against me would be met with failure—it would be.

Her level voice impressed me. "So, my goosebumps, which don't exist,"—*bullshit*—"are a physical manifestation of my attraction to you, which also doesn't exist." Bull fucking shit. "I take it the rumors of insanity running rampant in De Luca territory are true."

"Those aren't rumors. They're facts." I met her eyes and dared her to argue otherwise.

"Do you hate me?"

My eyes flicked back to the book, mostly to hide my surprise at her boldness. "Hate would require emotion, and I do not possess any of those where you are concerned." I adjusted my body, doing my best to be sure she couldn't see my pain. Angelo stopped hitting when welts began to form. His way of assuring no scars surfaced as evidence. It still hurt like a bitch.

"The hair on your forearms are raised."

So, the princess played games.

My lips tilted upward. I let it settle for a second before I tampered the smile. "Is that so?"

"It's a manifestation of your attraction to me."

"Possibly," I allowed, swallowing as I shoved down the thrill shooting through me. I didn't know what souls were made of, but in this moment, I suspected ours were the same. "It's certainly not natural."

And there we had it. The truth of my attraction, spoken out loud. Would she say something? Admit she lusted for me, too? Or let the opportunity slip through her fingers. Rational Damian knew this had to stop. Fuck-All Damian, who rose each time Angelo whipped me, didn't give a damn.

She didn't admit her attraction to me. But didn't stop this either.

Her eyes traced the way my fingers caressed the Dostoevsky pages. "Do you really think neuroses can physically present themselves?"

Most high school curricula didn't include Freud's "Dostoevsky and Parricide," so the fact that she recognized my references impressed me. Moreover, it built a bridge between us, and we stood at the center, wondering which side we'd walk to.

I flipped a page. "It makes more sense than the alternative."

"Not to me." She tucked her feet under her thighs, leaned against the cushion, and allowed herself to get comfortable.

I gave her the silence to think. Dostoevsky suffered from epilepsy. In Freud's essay, he argued Dostoevsky's epilepsy materialized after his father's death as a physical manifestation of his guilt over wishing for his father's death. I understood Dostoevsky wishing for his father's death—I felt the same way—yet I'd never feel guilt over it. Intentional or unintentional. But perhaps Renata was a better person than me. That wouldn't be a surprise.

I felt her eyes on me as she spoke. "Death should be a last resort. Not some trivial wish to be thrown about. And goosebumps, your example of emotions eliciting physical responses, aren't as severe as a condition like epilepsy."

I peered up from the novel and, for the first time since Ren had walked in, took in the sleeping shorts that exposed most of her legs and the satin spaghetti strap shirt, which hid nothing. Her nipples poked at the fabric, and my Adam's apple bobbed.

My eyes returned to her face. "Would you have stayed if I accused you of developing a heart condition over your attraction to me?"

She eyed where the throw blanket pressed against my hips. Maybe she did have goosebumps. "It wasn't an either-or situation. You weren't limited to goosebumps and cardiovascular disease."

"Perhaps." My hands untangled the blanket, flattened it as I held it open above the floor, and tossed it so it covered her body almost perfectly when it landed on her. "You overestimate my desire to converse with you."

"Which one of us was the first to speak?"

"If I recall, it was me... after I caught you sneaking around my room."

"You didn't catch me snooping. You caught me laying on your bed."

"Yet, you deny your attraction to me. Which is it, Knight? Are you attracted to me, or were you snooping?"

Probably both, now that I considered it.

"What is it with you and absurd either-or scenarios?"

I set the book aside and swiveled, so my feet touched the floor and my forearms rested on my knees as I leaned forward and hit her with a heavy stare. "Dodging my questions isn't going to earn you any respect from me, and seven days from now, when we start our senior year of high school, you'll be wanting that respect."

She met my actions, unfolding her legs and leaning forward, so mere inches separated our faces as we sat across from one another on the divans Mama and I once picked out together. "I have your respect."

"Is that so?"

"What do you call this?" She gestured between us. "Are you in the habit of discussing the psychology of literature with people you don't respect?"

Touché.

The pain in my back should have been a reminder to build higher walls. Instead, it torched them to the ground. The dangers of letting her see me in a vulnerable state didn't deter me, and something in her eyes begged me to believe she wasn't the enemy here.

Did she see my loneliness? Did she connect with it? It couldn't be fun stuck in that room all day.

I opened my mouth to speak, but she cut me off. "It's okay not to hate me. It's okay not to like me, too." She dipped her eyes to the blanket that had pooled at her lap before returning them to me.

Had it been wrong to give her the blanket? I was an asshole, yes, but Mama raised a gentleman.

My eyes followed hers to the blanket. "Hate would require emotions, and I—"

"—don't possess anywhere I'm concerned. Yeah, I got it. There's a difference between loneliness and solitude."

Her words reminded me of choice. I had two. I could be lonely, I could have solitude by choice, or I could chase the outlet she gave me. The cure. And I made my choice the next night, when I returned to the library, and we read *Infinite Jest* together and argued over the psychological consequences of having absent parents.

This isn't a big deal, I told myself as we walked back to our hall. *It's just an outlet. Just an outlet.*

I wondered what she told herself.

SEVEN

> "Trust is like a mirror.
> You can fix it if it's broken,
> but you can still see the crack
> in that motherfucker's reflection.
>
> — LADY GAGA

RENATA VITALI

I could ask myself what I was doing here a thousand times more, and I still wouldn't have an answer. Reading a book is like peeling the pages back on your soul. For eighty-thousand words, you become someone else. You bare yourself to the words, and you feel what the character feels. When you share that experience with another person, it's like sharing the same soul.

For the past three weeks, I'd been sharing the same soul with

Damiano De Luca. I didn't trust him. Hell, I barely even knew him, but there are people I've known all my life that I wouldn't trust to water my plants let alone spend night after night reading with.

Yet, like clockwork, when the clock beside my bed had turned to one a.m., I had slipped my sheets off and wandered down the hallway. Damian sat on the divan with a book in his hand and an identical copy for me. I eyed the paperback in his outstretched hand. *Atlas Shrugged.* Ayn Rand.

I took a seat but didn't touch the paperback. "No."

It was an impulsive reaction. A need to feel power after feeling so helpless in my decision to show up here. The best explanation I could come up with was, my father had taught me to build walls around myself. That included my heart, which seemed too interested in Damian for my own good. Attraction could be brushed off. But this need to seek company in him? Unshakeable.

Trust no one, I reminded my heart, then begged it to listen.

Damian laid the paperback beside him. "No?"

"Nope." I popped the P.

"Why not?"

I flummoxed for a reply. "It's in third person."

He looked unimpressed. "You read *The Brothers Karamazov* just fine."

My shoulders shrugged, and I tried my best to look like I wasn't pulling excuses out of thin air. "That was Dostoevsky. He's in another league."

"This is Ayn Rand."

"I can leave if you're committed to reading *Atlas Shrugged.*"

Damian stared me down. I wanted to give in, because yes, I was so damned lonely in that room all day. I couldn't afford another hour alone. It would drive me insane. As Damian stood, I almost backtracked, but I shut my mouth when I realized he was making his way to one of the shelves.

He pulled out a paperback and approached the divan. Junot Díaz. *The Brief Wondrous Life of Oscar Wao.* If anything, this made it worse. It meant he wanted me here just as much as I wanted to be here.

"There's only one copy. I'll read." Damian opened the book.

It was on the tip of my tongue to ask him why he was doing this. Instead, I swallowed the words down as he read. Damian had a voice like Zachary Webber's, and when he read in his light Texas accent, I swore he ruined me for audiobooks. No one could compare.

Stretched out on the divan at such a late hour, it was easy to fall asleep to Damian's voice. My eyes drifted shut. When I opened them again, he was carrying me down the hallway, his movements quiet and effortless.

I let out a yawn, my vision blurred from sleep. The darkness didn't help. When I shifted, Damian tightened his hold on me. So, I closed my eyes again and rested my head on his chest. He was supposed to hate me. I didn't trust him. I'd stolen his phone from him. I was a Vitali, and he was a De Luca.

But this didn't feel like hate.

191
189

EIGHT

> "The best way to find out if you can trust somebody is to trust them.
>
> — ERNEST HEMINGWAY

RENATA VITALI

Most schools have a mean girl. Devils Ridge High has three. Laura Willis. Maria Delgado. Adalasia Ricci. I'd clocked them the second I stepped into the hallway, my new schedule crumbled into a ball in my fist, already memorized.

They strut down the hall like a scene out of *Mean Girls*. Step. Hip sway. Step. Hair flip. Step. Wink. Step. Lucky for me, they gave me nothing more than narrowed eyes and thinly veiled jealousy. I encroached in their territory, still managing to draw attention despite the mess of clothes I wore.

My name protected me from bullying, and perhaps that drew the most resentment. Here I was, a privileged Vitali, the mafia princess they wanted to be. It was as glamorous as the title suggested, and yes, I had money, education, and status.

If that was your thing, I could understand the animosity. But my thing was wholesome families with parents who cared less about territorial disputes and more about the report cards I brought home each quarter.

This made me aloof. The I-don't-care expression made me easier to hate. The prestigious last name tacked onto my first? The nail on the green-faced coffin.

"Eyes up front, Miss Willis." The white-haired Mrs. Bruno flashed a warning look at Laura. Italian last name. All-knowing stare. Mafia-affiliated, I'd guess. Meaning, she knew the war going against me could start.

Laura swiveled in her seat, her eyes finally shifting away from me. I relaxed a little against the cheap plastic backrest and toned out of the AP Calculus BC lecture. I took it freshman year, and using derivates in growth and decay models didn't challenge me.

Instead, I cataloged the students in the classroom. Most took the phone ban seriously. Nearly everyone in this classroom sported pagers attached to their clothes. Laura, on the other hand, texted beneath the table each time Mrs. Bruno looked away. I added her to my mental list of potential candidates to steal a phone from. After all, I still needed to check my email to see if Maman had responded.

Damian came into the classroom ten minutes before class ended. No one said a word. Miss Willis greeted him with a smile and continued her lecture. He took a seat in the chair diagonally beside mine but didn't take out paper and a pen.

His body reeked of alcohol, and for all I knew, he'd been holed up in the local strip club or a brewery. We spent every night in the library together, yes, but we never talked about things that went on outside that room. I knew his dad beat him. He knew I needed company to chase away the loneliness. Beyond that knowledge, we kept things strictly book-related.

Except last night. I didn't know what last night was. Him covering his ass by making sure no one found me asleep in the library? But he could have just woke me up and let me walk myself back to my room. I was at a loss.

Damian turned his face to me and caught me staring. Sleep rimmed his eyes, and he mouthed, "Caught you," before he leaned his head on his desk and closed his eyes.

The bell rung, people filtered out of the classroom, but no one woke him up. I took my time gathering my things. Laura's frown stayed on her face as she strode out of the room, unhappy about my proximity with the school's 'It Boy' but unable to do anything.

Mrs. Bruno hesitated, looked between me and Damian, and left when she caught the unimpressed stare I gave the poor woman. In my defense, I needed privacy, it was rare to catch Damian at home, and our library was a sanctuary I didn't want to tarnish with anything but books.

"I know you're staring at me." His voice surprised me, but I tamped my reaction. I'd thought he'd fallen asleep.

I leaned against the desk and crossed my arms. "Is our time in the library wearing you out?"

"You don't wear me out, Princess."

"Knight," I corrected. Ugh, I hated being reminded that I was a mafia princess. "But you're worn out. Your shoulders are tense, and you can't shake the sleep from your eyes. We're in *public*." Fatigue was weakness, and weakness was not for public consumption.

"I know what you're thinking, but you're wrong. I'm alert, Princess. Agata wore a black cap. Backwards. Chuck Taylors. Isabella. White sundress. Flip flops. Braided hair. Brando. Black skinny jeans. White tee. Leather jacket. Gold chain. Pippa—"

"Okay, I get it. You're Shawn Spencer."

"And you're still here. Did you need something?"

It was like, as soon as we left the safe space of the library, civility fled. We stayed away from each other in public, but I couldn't help the concern, which crept into my body. I opened my mouth, a little fronted by the hostility.

Well, you stole his phone, Renata. What did you expect? For him to forget about it just because you spent some time in a library reading together?

An amused smile lined Damian's lips, and he stared at me like no one else before him. "I know you're concerned."

"I'm not."

"You are. It's cute, but it's not welcome. These people follow your family's rules because they're precedent and they won't survive a war against the Vitali nor domestic and international syndicates, but they've been bred to distrust you, Renata. If I'm seen with you, that distrust will extend to me."

Message received.

"Fine." I swallowed and tilted my chin up. "But if you're really concerned over the impression you give, you should fix whatever has you falling asleep in class." I swung my backpack over my shoulder, turned, and left.

I could have sworn I heard him mutter, "I'm trying."

Try not to be an asshole while you're at it.

> “For there to be betrayal,
> there would have to have been trust first.
>
> — SUZANNE COLLINS

DAMIANO DE LUCA

My best friend Cristian slid a package my way. “Here.”

Brown box. Plain. Nondescript.

A gift from The Benefactor.

I tore the package open. Five Gurkha cigars. Five instructions. Five more favors I owed a nameless devil. My fingers traced the hand carved camel bone chest before I lifted the lid. Taking the first in the set out of the packaging humidor, I drew it to my nostrils and inhaled.

Broadleaf Maduro. Cameroon binder. Aged Dominican filler. Sour, sweet, and twenty-three grand a box. Whoever The Benefactor was, he was wealthy and connected. These cases were rarer than a virgin escort.

I never smoked them—I didn't smoke or drink—but I didn't tell Cristian this as I pulled out an S.T. Dupont lighter, bought and paid for by centuries-old De Luca oil money. For now, he needed to think these cigars were just a gift and not secret messages.

Cris held his hand out. "We're in a five-by-five box, man. Control yourself."

I made a show of rolling my eyes before tucking the cigar back in the chest and leaning against the leather seat. "It's smoke, Cris. You'll live."

He ticked his fingers. "Formaldehyde, benzene, vinyl chloride, arsenic ammonia, and hydrogen cyanide. Some of many carcinogens in secondhand smoke."

I smirked. "Look who paid attention in health."

He shook his head and his dirty blond, surfer boy hair shook with it. "Stop giving me shit. We're in a box."

Hardly. We sat in a private room at The Landing Strip. Irene's room. Befriending Irene had been my first instruction from The Benefactor. She had the ins and outs of the club wired, and from intel to a debugged room to meet in, she had my back.

I didn't know how The Benefactor knew to single her out, but I'd made the decision long ago to take down my father. I was committed, and I would take all the help I could get. If The Benefactor posed a problem after I ascended the throne, I would take care of it then. I was a planner, but this was something I had little choice but to take one step at a time.

Cris nodded his thanks as I put away the cigars. He played his role well. The easygoing player no one could take seriously because they couldn't see past the charming smirk, half-assed pick-up lines, and laidback surfer style.

But time and time again, Cris had come through for me. There was no one I trusted more. When I take over the De Luca syndicate, I'll make him my senior advisor. Until then, he did the work I couldn't because leaving Devils Ridge would reveal my identity.

Right now, being unknown provided an advantage. Everyone here kept me a secret under Angelo's instructions, which he gave because he thought the less people who knew I existed, the less legitimate my chances at taking over the syndicate would be.

He was wrong.

I removed the cigar case from the shipping box and pushed the cardboard box to Cris. "Track this. Did you get a location on the last one?"

He grabbed the box from me, pulled a knife out of his pocket, and began cutting out the chunk of cardboard with the shipping information on it. A no name private company. He looked up at me midway. "Last package came from New York." He paused a beat. "Romano territory."

I watched as he finished his cutting. "Can you get an address?"

"I think my guy can get the origin city. Best we can do."

I nodded. "Thanks."

"Why do you think the Romano syndicate is sending you shit?"

"We don't know that it's the Romano syndicate."

"Who else?"

I shrugged and ran a hand over my face. "No clue, but it's a fancy gift, and clearly someone knows I exist."

"That should worry you. Today, it's fancy cigars—random outta fucking nowhere gift by the way. Tomorrow, it's poison in your lungs, bro."

"Yeah, but that's what tomorrow's for."

"You're a planner. You don't say things like that."

Lately, I was doing a lot of things I normally wouldn't. I didn't have a choice. I needed Angelo out of my life more than I cared about The Benefactor's motives. Everything unhinged Angelo, and I let him take out his anger on my back with his belt to buy me time, but one day, it wouldn't be enough. When that day came, I—or one of our own—would end up dead. I couldn't let that happen.

I studied Cris, eyeing the stress lines between his brows. "Do you trust me?"

"With my life."

"Then, trust me on this."

He heaved a sigh and nodded. "I have a package at my place, too. Amazon Prime, so I doubt it's a bomb or poison. But it was sent to my house, addressed to you. Kinda heavy. You think I should call in the boys to scan it?"

"No, it's clean."

The package was heavy because it was filled with textbooks. Six thicker than oatmeal textbooks for an ivory-skinned princess who hadn't come to the library for six days now. Fuck. Where was this guilt coming from?

I toyed with the cigar case in my hand and nodded to Cristian. "I'll pick it up tomorrow before school."

He cocked a brow. "And you're going to school, right?" When I nodded, he shook his head and grinned. "Just tell me who you're banging, dude. You know I'll pry it out of you. No one's interesting in this town, but it can't be the Vitali chick. She's hot, but she's a sloppy mess, and she never misses a class."

Renata was more than hot. She was fresh air slapping me in the face, better company than I knew was possible, and the goddamned cure to loneliness. She was also off limits, which I reminded Cris. "Renata is a Vitali, and Vitalis are off limits."

"If it's not the Vitali..." He tilted his head, narrowed his eyes, and grimaced. "Please, tell me it's not Laura."

"Hell, no." I wasn't banging anyone. I ditched a few classes and stayed out late most days to follow the instructions on the cigars, but again, I couldn't tell Cris. "I'll see you tomorrow morning."

He nodded, accepted the dismissal with ease, and stood. At the doorway, he turned and faced me. "Why are people sending shit to you through me?"

I did it because he lived alone. His dad was currently serving two life sentences in a supermax prison. I suspected The Benefactor had the same reasons. I just didn't know how he knew this much about my life.

"Because you're so popular."

Cris barked out a laugh, shook his head, and left. When the door shut, I plucked the first cigar from the case, unraveled it, and read the message, my mind reeling.

Look after the mafia princess.
I sent her to you for a reason.

Another secret revealed. Another secret to keep. I collected more secrets than a priest in a confessional.

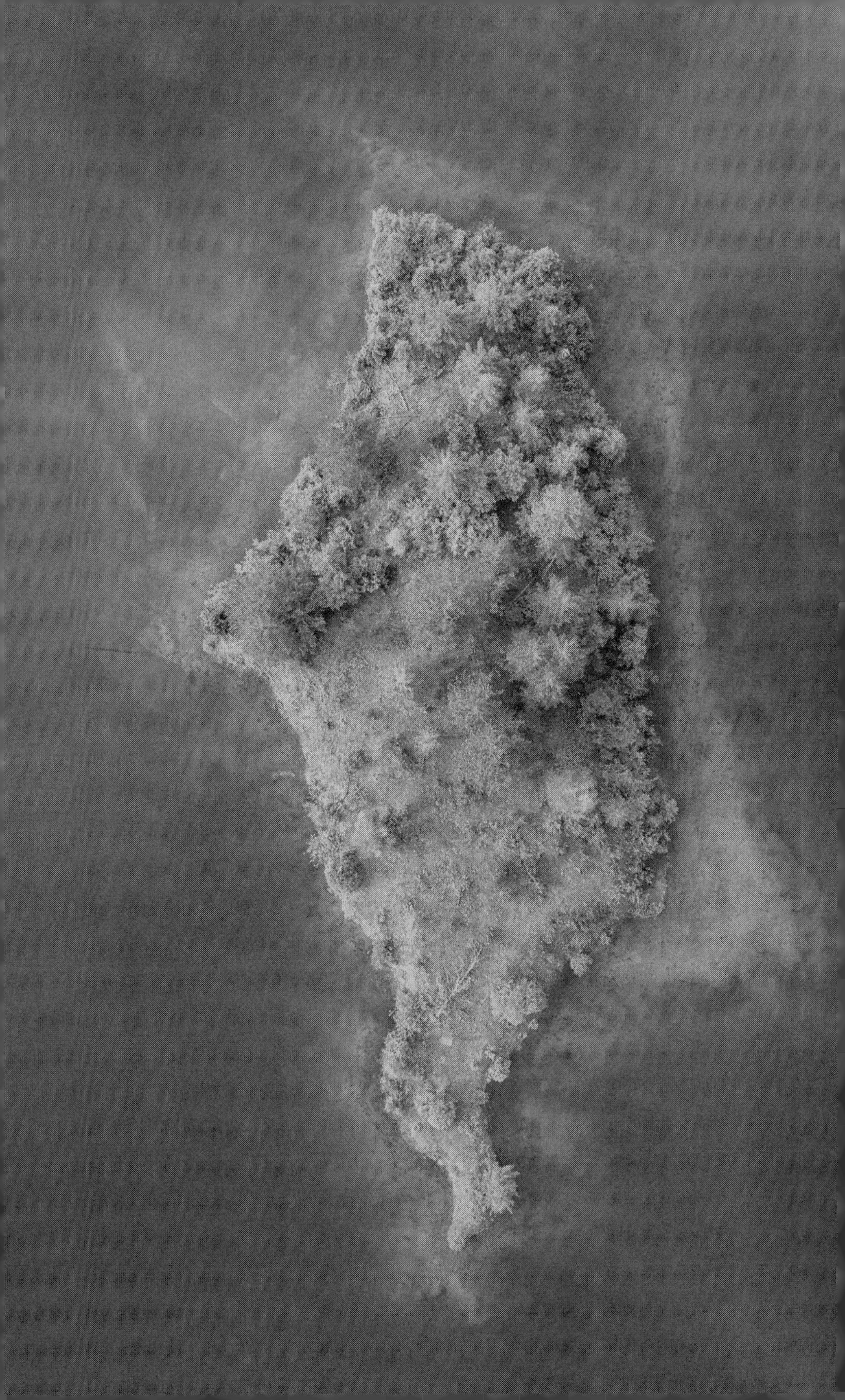

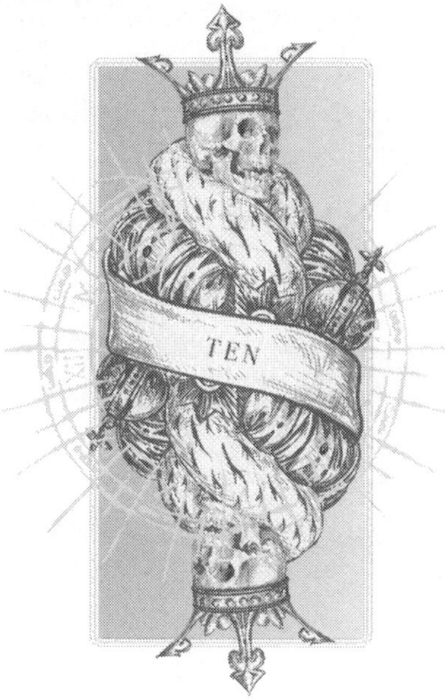

TEN

> To have faith is to trust yourself to the water.
> When you swim, you don't grab hold of the water,
> because if you do, you will sink and drown.
> Instead, you relax and float.
>
> — ALAN WILSON WATTS

RENATA VITALI

There's an island far off the coast of India, where a tribe of people live isolated. For thousands of years, they've lived with minimal contact with the outside world. They still practice hunting and gathering, make Stone Age weapons out of loose metals, and greet outsiders with arrows. Years of isolation bred distrust, and the sight of visitors is met with violence and hostility.

The De Luca syndicate reminded me of the Sentinelese. After

Ludovico De Luca killed his son, the Vitali and other syndicates wrote them off as crazy. Since then, they've lived isolated in their small territory of Arizona, New Mexico, Texas, and Oklahoma. No outside deals. No cross-territory agreements.

Hell, they're the only syndicate to never fight a war—and not because they aren't interested. No, because no one considers them worth it. And so, isolation bred distrust, and distrust turned into hostility and violence when it came to the Romano; Andretti; Rossi; Camerino; and most of all, the governing Vitali.

So, I wasn't surprised when I spent the first month of school without a single textbook. I squeezed by fine based on past knowledge, but it got exceedingly difficult the more assignments my teachers gave out of textbooks. In fact, I suspected some of them began giving book assignments to spite me.

Because like the Sentinelese, they treated me with hostility merely because I was a foreigner. They didn't trust me, and they certainly didn't trust the Vitali, which Damian outright admitted before he said he couldn't be seen with me.

So, I suffered. Assignment after assignment. Grade after grade. The library had magically run out of stock of every textbook I needed, I knew no one would lend me theirs, and I had no way of purchasing textbooks without access to the internet.

About a week after Damian told me we couldn't be seen together in person, I opened my locker to six brand new textbooks. One for each class I was taking. I stared at them, traced my finger along their spines, and wondered what the catch was. I'd move it, and a trip wire would cause a cascade of pig's blood to gush onto my head, à la *Carrie*. Or maybe I'd open one of them, and a horde of spiders would crawl out and attack me.

Either way, I didn't dare move them. At least not until the bell rung for first period, and the hallway cleared. The students scattered like ashes in the wind until only I remained in the hallway.

I reached into my pocket and pulled a pen out. Angling myself sideways in case something shot out of me, I stuck the pen in the locker and poked one of the books.

Nothing.

Another poke.

Still nothing.

"What are you doing?" The amusement in Damian's voice tickled my stomach when it should have put me on edge.

Wow, I was so bad at this grudge thing. Then again, a grudge implied I cared enough to hold one. Plus, Damian was awfully nonchalant for someone I had been avoiding for the past week.

I turned to face him, racked my brain for an explanation, and came up short, so I went with the truth. "There are new textbooks in my locker. I don't know who put them there, so I'm checking to see if they're boobytrapped."

He leaned against the row of lockers parallel to mine and crossed his arms. "Boobytrapped? This isn't *Home Alone*. We're not children fending off goons."

"I don't trust you guys." I trusted no one, except maybe my mom.

"They're just textbooks, Princess."

"How would you know that?"

He closed the distance between us and leaned against the locker next to mine. His breath fanned across my face as he inched forward, closing the gap between us. "Because I put them there." In one swift move, he swiped up the books and placed them in my hands with a raised brow. After giving me a two fingered salute, he turned and left.

I looked down at the textbooks, a little stunned. Calculus. Macroeconomics. Literature. Spanish. Environmental Science. Computer Science. My classes. He really made it hard to hate him. What was his end game?

Before he reached the door, he turned back to me. "And Princess?"

"What?"

"See you in the library tonight."

That.

That was his end game.

Maybe he needed me to chase away his loneliness as much as I wanted him to chase away mine. But damned if either of us would admit it.

ELEVEN

> "Loving someone is giving them the power to break your heart but trusting them not to.
>
> — JULIANNE MOORE

RENATA VITALI

A light switch has multiple components. A hot wire. A 120-volt AC current. A neutral white wire. Two terminals. Power running from the fuse box. It isn't just a switch. It isn't just turning something on or off.

Nothing is that simple.

This included turning the truce between me and Damian on and off. It'd be so simple to just hate him or like him but not both at the same time. That would be like Allied forces invading Normandy every morning and retreating every night.

It took a toll on me. I liked Damian when I shouldn't have and hated him when I could have allowed myself to like him. It was these conflicting emotions that distracted me as I wandered into the kitchen in the De Luca mansion.

I opened the fridge, which they had built into the antique cabinets, and pulled out a travel-sized bottle of orange juice. Araceli, who I suspected disliked me, had stopped delivering my breakfast, which left me to fend for myself out here.

When I shut the fridge door, Angelo stood on the other side, leering at me. "Little Miss Vitali, growing older and older each day, I see."

"You don't see anything, Angelo. You're blind." I rolled my eyes, uncapped the orange juice, and moved to walk around him.

His hand slammed down on the fridge, his arm now blocking my path. "You little—"

I cut him off before he could spew his stupidity. "—Do you not get it? Are you that daft? I can provoke you all I want. I can call you names. Throw punches. Hell… I can kill you, Angelo. I can reach out, grip your throat with my bare hands, and squeeze until the life drains out of your pathetic, beady eyes." I needed to nip this in the bud, to remind him of the hierarchy with words he could understand.

He pulled his gun out of his holster with his free hand and set it on the kitchen island. "Silly, naïve girl. I can end you right now. I can place a bullet in between your demon-red eyes and end this yapping before I get a fucking migraine."

I leaned on my heels and took a casual sip of my orange juice, which I knew would irritate him. "There's nothing you can do to stop me that won't end with you dead anyway. That's what it is to be a Vitali, and that's how little the De Luca name means."

His eyes narrowed, and he strode toward me. I started to question how much he cared about whether he lived or died. Maybe this was a bad idea. Maybe I wasn't providing a deterrent but giving him a challenge. Maybe instead of nipping this in the bud, I'd provoked him more. After all, rumors of the De Luca craziness had to exist for a reason, and he shared lineage with Ludovico De Luca.

"Your father thinks he can just send you into my territory without even consulting me. He thinks he owns the Italian mafia worldwide."—Papà policed it, which was close enough.—"He thinks he can do what he pleases, and all the other syndicates play along because that's how it's always been." His arm lowered from the fridge, and he took a step toward me. He reached out with his finger and poked me in the chest. "Well, he's wrong."—Poke.—"That's not how things happen in my territory."—Poke.—"You best tell your dad, the De Luca family answers. To. No. One." Poke. Poke. Poke.

I tilted my head. Condescension oozed out of me with purpose as I caught his finger between my fist. "I'd be happy to tell him that if you'd give me a phone." My saccharine smile escalated his rage.

Why wasn't I stopping? This was crazy. Angelo De Luca was a mad man, but I was mad, too. Last night, I'd seen the way Damian winced when laying on the library's divan. The day before that, I heard the whip of Angelo's belt through the air vent connecting my room to Damian's. My parents had odd ways of showing their love, but never once had they laid a hand on me.

Angelo slipped his finger from my grip and nodded at the gun. "There's a bullet in that gun with your name on it."

"Does that make you feel like a man? Do those threats help you sleep at night?" I took a step toward him, and I couldn't get a grip on my anger. My dad raised me to be the stereotypical calm Vitali, but I was so far from calm, I wouldn't be able to locate myself on a map. "Here's what helps me sleep at night. Knowing you're weak—"

"I'm not weak—"

"Only a weak man beats his son every night. You're alive because my family lets you live. You're alive because your son could beat you to a pulp but hasn't decided to capture your throne. It's that grace that has allowed the breath to flow through your lungs. One day, your luck will flee, and each breath you take will be a struggle. On that day, your son will lead your syndicate. I'll be there to laugh. And the rest of the syndicates will move on with their daily operations—no changes made, because you mean absolutely nothing to anyone."

I caught movement by the kitchen entrance. My eyes tangled with

Damian's over his dad's shoulder. Black and red. Red and black. No way out of this stare down but to dive deeper into this mess and trust I'd find an escape.

But a part me knew there was no escape.

TWELVE

> To be trusted is a greater accomplishment than to be loved.
>
> — GEORGE MACDONALD

DAMIANO DE LUCA

Tick. Tick. Tick.

I turned my metronome on and placed it on the floor in preparation for Angelo's visit tonight. The beat helped me focus, and I liked to concentrate on it instead of the whipping. And I had no doubt the whipping would be bad tonight. Angelo had to be mad after his show down with Renata, but he'd take it out on me.

I wasn't a push over. I didn't usually let people treat me like this. I'd always pictured fighting back throughout my childhood, but when I finally grew big enough to throw a mean punch, I had already set my eyes on dethroning Angelo. That was a job that would take more than brute force and a few clever punches.

So, I sucked it up. I held my anger in. And every night, like clockwork, Angelo came into my room, slid his ten-thousand-dollar snake skin belt from his pant loops, and went to town on my back, stopping just before the skin split to avoid physical evidence.

The door opened. I laid flat on my bed, not bothering to look up. His belt made noise as he unbuckled it. It slid across his pants, and still, I didn't look.

His bored tone did nothing to abate my irritation. "Kneel. Floor. You know the drill."

I realized I must have looked absurd, too damn old and big to let anyone beat me like this and not fight back. But I did as Angelo demanded, my mind blank. My knees met the floor. The wood dug into my skin. Still, no noise but the metronome.

A whip of the belt.

Tick.

Another.

Tick.

More, more, more.

Tick. Tick. Tick.

The raw skin on my back blistered. This was about the time he would usually stop, but he kept going.

"You're a disrespectful bastard."

Whip.

"I never wanted you."

Whip.

"You'll be nothing."

Whip.

I rolled my eyes and stared at the metronome on the floor.

Tick. Tick. Tick.

Whip. Whip. Whip.

His words no longer made sense, his insanity growing wilder and wilder each time the snake skin connected with my flesh. He hadn't always been like this. When Mama lived, he kept to himself while she raised me. When she died, he took it as permission to have his way with me. Never leaving a scar. Hitting just enough to take me to the brink of bloodied flesh.

But my skin split today, and I knew Renata's words—true as they were—had done a number on him. Fuck my life. The belt sliced the skin below my shoulder. I grit my teeth. Didn't she know she'd made it worse?

He growled out, his Texas accent strengthening with his fury. "No fucking respect in my own fucking household. I own the De Luca family." *Whip*. "I own this land." *Whip*. "I own this town. I own this state." *Whip*. *Whip*. "Do you get that, boy?"

Not for long, he didn't.

I didn't answer. He tore the skin on my lower back. My teeth drew blood from my tongue. Any more lashes, and I'd need a hospital trip for stitches. He didn't relent, the belt whipping in rapid succession.

Each time someone challenged Angelo's ego, he took it out on me. I was the threat to his throne, the only De Luca in the line of succession, the only one who could take over. That made me his target, and if he could kill me without incensing the entire town, he would.

Instead, he settled for a belt and my back, and I let him because I was biding my time until the cogs fell into place and I gathered enough supporters, turned his *caporegimes* and soldiers against him, and could guarantee a successful coup. He sought short reprieves; I planned for the end game.

Angelo pushed me forward with the heel of his boot on my back. I let him, my eyes shifting to my dresser, where I knew a pen laid. A lunge forward. A swipe of the hand. A click of the pen. A push deeper, deeper, deeper into his neck, and Angelo would bleed out while I watched. I didn't do it, but I considered it for point five seconds before I reminded myself of my grand plan.

The Benefactor's plan.

Spend time with the lower level De Lucas at The Landing Strip. Treat them better than Angelo ever could. Work my way up to converting the *caporegimes*. Use my army to dethrone Angelo and his loyalists. And keep Angelo alive to watch the syndicate he could never wrangle thrive under my rule.

My face pressed against the cool wood. A final lash on my back severed another strip of my skin. The blood on my tongue pooled in my mouth. *Tick. Tick.*

"Look at you, taking a beating like a weak, pathetic, little bitch." He really had no idea. His guffaw sounded too jovial for the blood dripping down my back. "You're no son of mine." The tip of his boot connected with the back of my head, whipping it to the side.

The last image I conjured before darkness faded in was the fall of Angelo De Luca.

> "Trust yourself.
> You know more than you think you do.
>
> — DR. BENJAMIN MCLANE SPOCK

RENATA VITALI

I wasn't sure Damian would show up at the library that night, but he'd beat me to it. By the time I had a copy of Kahlil Gibran's *The Prophet* open, Damian had fallen asleep on the divan opposite of mine.

My eyes crawled the length of his body, studying him in a way I normally couldn't. At six-two, his legs hung off the edge, and his muscular frame hardly fit the divan. He had an arm slung over his head, pulling the bottom of his shirt up. I caught a peak of the V leading into his sweats and bit my lip. *Holy hell.* They didn't make men like him in Connecticut.

"You're not reading." I jerked my attention back to his face. His eyes still remained closed, and he looked like he was sleeping. He peeked an eye open. "If you're not going to read, what's the point?"

My brows drew together, and I pulled the book closer to my chest. "I didn't think you'd be here."

The anger I'd seen on his face in the kitchen still lingered in my mind. I'd been wrong to intervene in his life like that, but I didn't regret it. Not as much as I should have. Angelo De Luca needed to be taken down a peg or ten.

"Are we not doing this anymore?"

I wanted to ask what exactly *this* was. But that would cross an unspoken line, so I sighed, drew my knees to my chest, opened *The Prophet*, and started to read. Damian's breathing leveled out again as I read him to sleep.

My eyes darted between the page and his body as I read, "The timeless in you is aware of life's timelessness. And knows that yesterday is but today's memory and tomorrow is today's dream."

"Do you have any dreams?" His words jolted me. Not just because I'd thought he was asleep, but because his question went to a place I thought we'd never go.

We never talked like this. Sure, we would talk about things like absentee parents, but we wouldn't talk about what it felt like for *us* to have absentee parents. That line I didn't want to cross? He'd just crossed it with both feet.

I bit back a sigh. "Yes." I dreamed of loving parents, a normal life, a room full of books, and someone to share them with. It struck me that an unbiased observer would say I had the last two. The idea scared me, so I blurted out, "I dream of leaving this place. Getting the hell out and running as fast as I can."

"Running away?"

"Yes."

His eyes remained closed, his arms clasped together atop his stomach. "Small words for someone used to speaking big ones."

If anything, I thought he felt the same way. How could he live with Angelo De Luca and not want to run away?

I brushed my hair out of my face and stared at his closed eyes and the slow rise and fall of his chest. "What do you mean?"

"I'm referring to the way you speak to my father, and you know it."

"Oh."

"It's not a good idea to talk to him like that."

"I know."

"If you think you're doing me any favors, you're wrong. What do you think happens after all that? You rile Angelo up, and he has no way of simmering down. He's not made like you and me. He's a boiling pot with his lid superglued on tight. *We* can lift our lids. *We* can let the steam out. *We* can release our anger. He can't. Not until he reaches a crux, and someone gets hurt."

"Who got hurt?" I reexamined him again, noting the way he laid over three plush blankets, his body more rigid and less relaxed than I'd initially thought. His leveled breathing? Not sleep, but rather a way to prevent him from moving and exacerbating his injuries. "Oh. I-I—" I didn't know what to say, but the sound of Angelo beating his son echoed in my head.

He saved me from answering by standing up. His movements drew a wince, but he tampered it. My jaw dropped a bit when I caught sight of the crimson soaking the sides of his gray shirt, stretching into the back.

My eyes dipped to the divan. Violent red stained one of the blankets. I wouldn't be surprised if it had soaked through the three thick blankets and into the black fabric of the divan. For the life of me, I couldn't figure out why he'd come here. To the library. To me.

He faced me, his eyes never wavering from mine as one hand clutched the front of his shirt. His fingers tugged the shirt over his head. Chiseled abs met my gaze, but I didn't dare focus on them. I watched in sheer horror as he tossed his shirt to the side and turned around, his movements slow and no doubt painful.

Angry pink crisscrossed lines littered his back. Dried blood decorated some, but others still bled. Trails of red ran down his back in streams like scattered rain drops.

I shook my head and begged him with my mind to spin his back away from me. "Why haven't you washed the blood away?"

He turned around and arched a brow at me. "It's on my back. I can't reach it myself. Hospital trips aren't an option. The closest one is the next town over, and there aren't many De Luca contacts there. I'd need someone to make arrangements just to head over."

This. This was how the De Luca syndicate had kept Damian a secret all these years. He stayed in Devils Ridge, a town with nearly a hundred-percent mafia ties. They kept his secret because they belonged to the syndicate, and the Vitali and other four syndicates would never spy because they'd long ago written off the De Luca family.

I shook my head. "So, make them. Unless Angelo won't let you, in which case, fuck him. Let the bastard rot in jail."

"He'd be out in a heartbeat."

"But you'd have medical attention. The marred gashes on your back will scar, Damsel." I realized my slip a second too late. I was supposed to call him Day. Anything—literally anything—but Damsel.

"Damsel?" He took a step toward me, steel in his eyes. "I'm the Damsel, and you're the Knight? Do you think you're brave antagonizing Angelo, Knight?" The mocking way he spit out 'Knight' provoked me.

Deep down, I knew I shouldn't have said anything to Angelo. It was a mistake, one I'd realized too late. But I stood my ground anyway. "Someone had to."

"No, Renata." He shook his head, something like disgust in his eyes. "That's exactly the kind of behavior I'd expect from Angelo, not someone who argues Apollonian and Dionysian in the context of *The Birth Tragedy* in ways that would put Nietzsche to shame."

How did he manage to make me feel so ashamed of myself?

My head dipped down, and I stared at the rug my toes dug into. "Can you put your shirt back on?"

"Why? The consequences of your actions too much for you to handle?"

I ignored his provocation. I just couldn't look at the welts anymore. He'd turned, but I still caught some lashes on his sides.

"Please," I begged.

He stared at me for a moment before moving. Slowly. So slowly. His knees were partially bent, his arms outstretched to his shirt on the ground, when I said, "Wait."

"Yes?"

I bent over, grabbed his shirt, then reached for his hand. I knew if I told him where I planned on taking him, he'd deny me. So, I led him to the bathroom in our hall, walking slowly to accommodate his back.

"Princess—"

I opened the door. "Let me help you."

"Like you helped by talking to Angelo?"

"I'm sorry, okay?! I was mad."

He let loose a bitter laugh. "What I don't get is why. You're normally unfazed. You're the girl who stole my phone without blinking an eye—"

"I didn't steal—"

He cut off my denial. "You're not the girl who gets mad."

I tossed his shirt to the ground, grabbed a hand towel, and dipped it in the bathing pool to soak it. "I hear him. Every night, when he comes to your room, I can hear him through the air vent separating our rooms. Don't flatter yourself and think my anger is for you. If it were anyone else taking the beating, I would be angry for them, too. I may keep my calm well, but that doesn't mean I'm not allowed to feel empathy."

"Let me make this clear, Princess. I don't need your help."

"Fine. Point taken. But let me clean your wound."

His eyes dipped to the wet towel in my hand. "You have ten minutes."

My eyes traced his tanned skin. The hard ridges of his abs. The way his biceps bulged. He was cut like a warrior, lean but ripped, and he'd let his father tear him up. I didn't understand it.

"Why don't you fight back?" I pressed the towel against his back, forcing myself to continue when his body went rigid.

"Stay out of my business, Vitali."

Fine. Fair enough. He didn't trust me, and I didn't trust him. Message received. Instead of talking to him, I focused on my work. The fresh blood was easy enough to clean, but the dried blood wouldn't let up. I could rub at it, but that would be painful for him.

"Do you have hydrogen peroxide?"

He shook his head. "No."

My eyes drifted to the pool. "Take off your pants."

"Listen, you're attractive, but—"

Good Lord, have mercy.

"No, I mean take off your pants, so you can soak the dried blood off."

I turned the water heater on, and when I turned around, he'd barely gotten his pants a few inches down. I couldn't image the pain he was in. Without a word, I pushed his hands to the side and slid his pants slowly down his legs. Neither of us said anything as I squatted, fully aware of the intimate view. His boxers would have to remain, or I wouldn't be able to get anything done.

When I stepped back, his eyes stayed on mine as I slipped my shirt over my head. Back when Angelo had walked in on my bath, Damian hadn't bothered to stare at my body. Today, he was shameless in his perusal.

His hooded eyes crawled their way down my body, relentless in the way he watched me slide my sweats down my legs until I stood in front of him in black lace panties and a matching bralette. The only cute things I ever bothered wearing.

If anything, he inspected me on purpose. To make me as uncomfortable as I was sure accepting help from me made him. I watched him step into the bathing pool. He had to be in pain, but he didn't show it. Stoic as ever.

This shouldn't have been erotic, but my heart battered my chest as I waded to him. He watched me, his attention so focused on me as I stepped around him until I stood at his back. Cupping water into my hands, I let it run down his skin. After a few repetitions, the dried blood began to clear.

His muscles tensed as I ran my hand down them. For the first time ever, I felt truly off kilter. I pushed my emotions out of my mind and grabbed a bottle of shampoo.

"What are you doing?"

I popped the bottle open and squeezed some onto my hand. Forming a lather, I ran my hands over his head. His skin felt hot against my fingers. "I'm betting you haven't showered, and you won't be able to lift your hands high enough to wash your hair for at least another day."

I'd expected him to fight me on this, but he didn't. So, I massaged the shampoo into his hair, taking longer than necessary. My toes pointed as I used them to push me higher, trying but struggling to reach his head. My chest nearly bumped into his wounds, so I stepped back and walked to his front.

From this angle, we couldn't avoid staring at each other as I ran my hands through his hair. I still stood on my tiptoes, but this time, he helped me. His arm wrapped around my back, and he held me still against his chest. My nipples pebbled beneath my bralette. They pressed against his bare chest through the thin fabric.

His breath fanned my face as I massaged his scalp. He closed his eyes. I took the opportunity to study him. The distinct jawline. The high cheekbones. He could be a model or a movie star if he fled this town, ran away from this mafia life, like I'd always wanted to.

"I'm sorry," I whispered. "It's hard to hear. Okay? Every night, it's hard to hear."

He said nothing. I cupped water into my palms and poured it over his head. When the water ran clear, I stepped back.

His eyes shot open. "I need you to do something for me."

"Okay." I figured I owed him as much.

"Make sure I don't fall asleep. I could have a concussion."

"He hit your head?"

"Kicked it. On the side. My hair hides it. No bruises that way."

"He can't get away with this."

"He won't."

And if I wasn't so focused on his pain and how close we stood, I would have realized what his words meant. Damian had a plan to get back at Angelo. Maybe even take him down. That was treason, and he'd just confessed it to me.

Trust.

He trusted me, and I didn't even realize it.

FOURTEEN

> “In the end,
> you have to choose whether or not
> to trust someone.
>
> — SOPHIE KINSELLA

DAMIANO DE LUCA

Now that you’re friends with Miriam, she will bring her dad to you when the abuse gets too big to hide from him. They’ll ask you for help. You’ll convince them that dethroning Angelo is the only way.

I'd gotten the message from The Benefactor exactly two weeks after Renata arrived in Devils Ridge. I waited. Waited. Then, waited some more. I almost thought The Benefactor had gotten something wrong when Miriam and her father ambled their way into The Landing Strip.

The dark club shadowed Miriam, but I could see the shiner burgeoning on her eye. The closer she came, the more bruises I caught. She hid them with makeup and long sleeves, but I'd gotten good at recognizing abuse.

When they approached me, I stood and led them to Irene's private room. The three of us sat on the leather, neither Miriam nor her dad Manuel talking.

I took pity on them. "He hit you again."

My dad's advisor Jacapo was a real nasty piece of work. When I was ten, he'd walked in on my father beating me and stayed to watch. It wasn't a stretch to assume he was responsible for Miriam's bruises.

Manuel glanced at his daughter before returning his gaze to me. "Yes. I don't know how long Mir's been hiding this from me, but even a second is too long." His voice caught, and he paused. "It's too long, Damian."

"For what it's worth, I'm sorry this is happening to you, Miriam. You deserve better. But the options here are slim. If you flee, Jacapo will find you. If you kill him, you'll end up in jail or Angelo will kill you both."

Miriam tugged at the collar of her dress, a nervous tick I'd noticed a while back. "We were hoping you could go to your dad, and..." Her voice trailed off as I stood, turned around, and lifted my shirt. Her gasp echoed in the small room. "Oh, my God. Damian."

It felt bittersweet to show my scars. People saw scars as vulnerability, but these were my choice. I let Angelo hit me. Not because I was weak, but because I could take it while I waited for my plan to fall into place.

I also found justice in using the scars Angelo gave me against him. They would be a useful tool in converting more De Luca members, starting with Miriam and Manuel. But I couldn't go around lifting my shirt without cause. It would raise suspicions.

Maybe later, Angelo would slip up again and leave a mark somewhere visible. Somewhere people couldn't ignore. Like a black eye people would ask me about and I could "reluctantly" attribute to Angelo. Show them how unhinged he'd become to his own son. Show them that, if they stepped wrong, this could be them unless I dethroned Angelo.

"Son—"

I was no one's son, and I needed to make that clear. "I'm not showing this to garner sympathy. I'm showing you both my scars to show you the type of man Angelo is. If you go to him and tell him that Jacapo has been beating Miriam, he will not behave like another syndicate boss would."

Manuel shook his head. "But—"

"He's stuck in a different era, Manuel."

"The other syndicates—"

"—have changed. Women are treated equally. They aren't dismissed. The syndicates rarely resort to violence to resolve issues."

Miriam's eyes widened, and tears brimmed in them. "Why can't that be us? Dad?"

Manuel turned to me. This was good. Yes, he'd been an obedient soldier all his life and perhaps looking for leadership in others came naturally, but the fact that he looked to me instinctually coupled with how well-liked he was in this syndicate made him a great ally. The Benefactor had been right. Again.

I reached out and touched Miriam's shoulder. "The De Luca syndicate will remain the same so long as Angelo De Luca remains the same."

"I-I..." Manuel reached out, squeezed his daughter's hand, and cleared his throat. "I'm at a loss for what to do here. If we can't leave and we can't stop Jacapo, what do we do?"

I didn't respond, instead waiting for them to come to the conclusion first.

A few minutes of silence passed before a hesitant Miriam stood up and turned to us both. Her eyes were a bit feverish, and she either looked determined or unhinged. "We take Angelo De Luca down."

"Honey…" Manuel sent an uncertain look my way. "We can't talk like this."

"Dad, look what Jacapo did to me. Look what Angelo did to Damian. We can do this. The three of us can do this." She turned to me. "You're his son. You're the only one who can take over. Please, Damian. I'm your friend. Please."

And there we had it. I'd gotten her to beg me for what I wanted in the first place. Manipulation never felt good, especially when it came without much effort.

I took a few minutes to respond, making a show of my hesitation. "We would need to turn people to our side."

Manuel's head peeped up, hope transforming his features. "What do you need us to do? Anything."

"Right now, people in this town are convinced Angelo De Luca is good for them." I'd been slogging my way through people, turning them away from Angelo step by step. There was still a considerable amount of people on the fence, and Manuel's support would be the difference. "We need to convince them otherwise."

Miriam nodded. "My dad has many friends that are soldiers and *capos*. I am friends with all the girls here, and their clients are all syndicate."

"You'd need to be careful. Subtle."

"I will. I can do it."

And I believed her. Hell, The Benefactor must have believed her, too, or we wouldn't be here.

I continued, "Some people will be on the fence. I can't just show them my scars."

"Why not?"

Manuel answered for me. "It's suspicious. He can't walk around without a shirt. People who cut, for instance, hide their scars. People will wonder why he's not hiding them. Why now? If they ask those questions, it can be dangerous."

I nodded. "I'll need Angelo to hurt me where people can see. A black eye. Something on my face. Sleeves can cover arms. Pants can cover legs. It has to be the face."

"And you can do this?"

I thought of Ren. She'd said it was difficult to hear me get beaten, and here I was, plotting more abuse. Hell, she'd just washed my scars, and now I was planning more marks. As soon as I realized I was even considering her, I pushed the thoughts of her away.

This was *my* syndicate.

This was *my* future.

It was the future I wanted.

... And it didn't involve Renata Vitali.

FIFTEEN

> Trusting is hard.
> Knowing who to trust, even harder.
>
> — MARIA V. SNYDER

RENATA VITALI

Time passed oddly in Devils Ridge. Days seemed to drag, but nights passed too quickly. When it came to our nights in the library, they couldn't come fast enough. Weekdays were easier. I had school to monopolize my time until the De Luca driver dropped me back off at the mansion, and I spent the rest of the day doing homework, taking naps, and waiting for one in the morning to come.

Weekends were the worst. I had no electronics, I saved reading for my library nights with Damian, and I could only sleep so much. There was nothing to do to pass time. Damian spent most of the weekends out of the house.

But this week, Angelo left for Oklahoma to seal another oil deal, and I hadn't heard Damian leave his room. The housekeepers even dropped off his breakfast and lunch to his door. Still, neither of us approached the other. I spent the day lying in bed, mostly staring at the ceiling. In silence. So much silence.

In the jungle, silence is a sign of danger. Animals know to stay silent when a predator comes. The mafia world is a lot like the jungle, and I should have considered this with each passing second.

And then I heard it.

The first grunt.

I thought I was hearing things at first, but then it happened again. The sound came from the wall Damian and I shared. I sprung out of bed and inched closer. Another grunt. Dragging the nightstand to the air vent, I stood on it.

Angelo wasn't here. This couldn't be a beating. And when I peeked through the vent and caught a blurred image of Damian in bed, I knew it was definitely not Angelo. I couldn't make out a clear image through the vent, so I scrambled off the nightstand and onto the bed.

I pulled the covers over me as if they'd protect me from the image spearing my brain.

Another grunt, but this time, he added, "Fuck, yes."

A feminine moan filled my room, and she panted out, "Yes, Daddy. Faster."

Damian groaned out, "Feels so good."

I ducked my hand beneath my sheets and toyed with the trim of my panties. I was going to Hell. Damian moaned again, and my fingers dipped below the fabric, teasing my clit. Listening to Damian with another woman shouldn't have hurt me, but it did. It gutted me. Still, I couldn't stop touching myself.

"Yes, please. Faster. Faster. Faster. I'm so close."

Dear Lord, there were two of them.

Two. Girls.

That gut-punch feeling could go to Hell. I didn't own Damian. No,

I didn't even want him. *Right?* But the sounds of his grunts hitched my breath, and driving away this lust seemed impossible. I tried to push it out of my head, wondering what the hell I was doing.

"Harder," one of the girls begged.

I slid two fingers inside of me and pictured Damian above me. His hand was on my breast, my neck, my hair, his scent everywhere. I was close. I could hear him groaning from his room, too, and I came. Breathy. Moaning. Way too loud.

Definitely going to Hell.

My cheeks burned as I came down from the high, unable to believe what I'd just done. I made a mess on my hand, so I slid off the bed to sneak across the hall to the bathroom. Damian's door opened the same time mine did.

I considered pretending I hadn't seen him before deciding that would be too obvious. I turned to face him and crossed my arms. "Your dad has a ban on guests, and I wouldn't piss him off. Not that you're around to see it, but he's been on a rampage lately."

His eyes flattened, and he skimmed them over my body. "Has he hurt you?"

"No." I peeked around him, trying to peer into the room as subtly as I could.

"There's no one in the room, Princess."

"But I heard—" I faltered, not liking how pathetic I sounded. "There was a girl—"

"Porn, Princess. It was porn. You've never watched it?" His amusement had me reconsidering the past twenty minutes. He knew I could hear him through the vent. Had he done this on purpose?

I shook my head. "I heard—"

A smirk lined his lips. "It's called jacking off. You know, self-pleasure. Masturbating. Cleaning your rifle."

"Okay, I get it."

"Painting the ceiling. Playing the skin flute. Choking the cyclops."

"Damian."

"Milking the lizard. Dishonorable discharge. Croaking the frog."

"Oh, my God."

"Firing the flesh musket. Giving a dirty handshake. Basting the ham."

"I swear to God—"

"—Taking the sausage hostage. Emptying the cache. Clearing my browser history."

"You like to touch your penis. I get it."

If it were anyone else, they'd be laughing at his words. Neither of us laughed, even when we poked fun and prodded one another's buttons. Damian sobered. The silence between us reminded me of the jungle. Except he was the predator, and he'd already *come*.

"Angelo will return later today." Damian's eyes ran over me once more, methodical and almost detached in their perusal of my body. As if cleaning him in the bath had never happened. And then he said the most unexpected thing. "If my dad tries to hurt you, find me."

It was little things like this which told me he cared.

And it was the pathetic pattering of my heart which told me I did, too.

SIXTEEN

> "Love meant jumping off a cliff
> and trusting that a certain person would be there
> to catch you at the bottom.
>
> — JODI PICOULT

DAMIANO DE LUCA

"I think it's unrealistic. Impossible, even."

Who knew, between the two of us, Princess would be the pessimist and I, the idealist?

I eyed the article of great-great-grandfather Ludovico on the wall, careful to keep my eyes off of Ren. I was well aware that I enjoyed our nightly literary debates way too much. "You don't think people have the innate goodness in them to rally for a common goal?"

The magazine felt heavy in my hand. Not because it was an issue of Playboy, nor because it was a limited edition 1984 run, but because it was the only thing keeping me from striding across the library's timber floors and kissing Princess. Vitali blood or not, I wanted her. Craved her in ways I'd never allow myself to pursue. She was, after all, a Vitali. And I was, after all, a lowly De Luca prince.

"Think about it like this. Decent people don't commit hardcore crimes, nor do they always follow the rules. They sneak into the carpool lane or speed when they shouldn't, but they're not out there murdering people. They don't go out of their way to donate all their non-basic essentials, but every once in a while, they'll volunteer at the local animal shelter. They're just... normal. Balanced. Trying to live their lives as best as they can, but sometimes their best isn't *the* best." She sat on the divan across from me and set her copy of *The Toynbee Convector* down.

Her eyes darted to my *Playboy*, which held the original copy of the short story we were discussing. "Say there's a normal distribution of goodness in the world, and the average person, at 50%, is a decent person. That would mean there are 34% of less-than-decent people, 13.5% of bad people, and 2.5% of awful people. That's billions of people that aren't even decent. You think *they* could muster up all that gushy goodness to create a utopia based on the crazy rantings of a self-proclaimed time traveler?"

"Fucking hell." I shook my head, ignoring how hot her arguing made me. I wanted to pry that paperback from her hands and replace it with my body. "Did you really just ruin Ray Bradbury for me?"

"Maybe you should learn to debate better."

"Maybe *you* should learn to—"

My dad's voice rang in the hallway as he yelled at one of the maids. Ren's disappointed eyes met mine before we both scanned the room. She scrambled upward and slipped behind the nearest floor-to-ceiling drape, hiding like we were doing something wrong by spending time with each other. Maybe we were, but it didn't feel wrong until someone invaded our bubble.

"Ah, there you are, my prodigious son."

I turned to Angelo as he swung the double doors open, and they struck the doorstoppers. "Obviously." I paused a beat, a carefree smirk I didn't feel curving my lips. "I didn't think you knew what 'prodigious' meant, but hey, I didn't think you could find the library either."

"Shut your fucking mouth or your biggest life accomplishment will be cleaning toilets at The Landing Strip."

My dad owned The Landing Strip, the one and only strip club in Devils Ridge, but he didn't know I frequented the place. Not for enjoyment, but to network. To show the De Luca soldiers and *caporegimes* how they could be treated if they supported me.

And I *had* cleaned the toilets there. I helped the staff, got my fucking hands dirty, made jokes with them on their breaks, asked them about their sons and daughters, and showed them just how much more I cared for them than my father did. Just one of my many steps to dethroning Angelo.

I dipped a hand into my pocket and leaned a hip on one of the divans. "What do you want?"

"You see the Vitali girl lately?" He sneered and whistled at the same time, which was kind of impressive if you thought about it. "She's growing."

I leaned further against the cushion and forced myself to remain impassive. "You're sick."

Angelo took a seat on the divan closest to where Ren hid. "There's an opening at The Landing Strip."

"And?"

"And it's time we made that Vitali girl earn her keep." Behind my dad, the drape shifted. Ren must have been pissed, or creeped out, or both.

"Earn her keep? You've been cooped up in this town too long, old man." I eyed Ren's copy of *The Toynbee Collector* beside him. "That idiom no longer refers to room and board."

"What?"

"Never mind." I ran a hand down my face and contemplated the millions of things that could be running through Ren's mind right now. "Seriously, what do you want?"

"The Vitali girl working at The Landing Strip."

I couldn't be related to Angelo.

Just fucking couldn't be.

He was the sperm that should have been swallowed.

And I was his offspring.

What did that make me?

The muscles in my neck tightened. "She's a minor, and she's a Vitali. Either of those reasons alone should be enough to dissuade a rational person fit for the position of De Luca mafia boss."

He ignored my dig—just barely, I suspected. "The Vitali need to know their place."

"What do you think happens when a minnow picks a fight with sharks?"

My dad stood up, his fists clenched at his sides. "Watch your mouth, son."

I had been.

For eighteen fucking years, I had been.

But I felt my plan coming to fruition, and I needed him to lose control for it to work. I needed him to take a swing at me and make contact. Somewhere visible, where the physical proof couldn't be missed. A black eye, perhaps.

"Oh, Angelo. You don't get it, do you?" I shook my head and *tsked*. "You're the minnow. The Vitali are the sharks. And they will eat you alive." I rose from the divan until we stood eye-to-eye, arms width apart. "Feel free to facilitate your own death, but leave the De Luca name out of your mess."

"You will not disrespect me like this."

"I already have." I'd always taken his abuse without a word, and maybe he'd gotten used to it because his eyes expanded before forming angry slits. Still, he needed more provocation. I let loose a deep, disrespectful chuckle. "Or what, Dad? You gonna kill me like Great-great-grandfather Ludo killed his son? I dare you to fucking try."

Hatred brimmed in me, such a contrast from my time spent with Ren, and with her mere feet away, I wanted to stand up for myself. I didn't want her to see me like this. Didn't want the patience I needed to take over the syndicate to coerce me into taking the emotional abuse my dad had been spewing my way since childhood. Didn't want to wait for this damned plan to work before I destroyed him.

But I needed him to punch me. I needed there to be physical proof of him losing control for the soldiers and *capos* to see. An inkling of doubt lurked in my conscience. Ren didn't need to hear this.

Too late.

Dad swung at me, his form all brute and no finesse. I feigned a dodge to maintain appearances of a fight but let his fist connect with my face. It connected hard enough to leave a bruise. He adjusted his suit while I fell to the floor. As he towered over me, a sharp laugh struck the air before he walked away.

I leaned my head back onto the floor, thinking about the million times he had dished a similar punishment to me. Usually with a belt on my back. This time around, the marks would be visible. This was what I wanted, wasn't it?

Self-pity clogged my throat, making the breaths I forced myself to take sluggish. A few seconds after the door clicked shut, Ren emerged from behind the drape and stared at me. She moved a step closer, and a lock of hair loosened from her bun and covered her right eye. Didn't matter. I had the color memorized.

She looked particularly angelic in that moment, though. The light blonde hair. Pale skin. Eyes an inhuman shade of amber. But I preferred her naughty side. The one that argued with me—all strength, backbone, and sass. I wondered which side she'd give me now.

I waited for her to say something. The more time passed, the more I convinced myself she'd rub what had happened in my face. Self-pity didn't flatter me, but I did nothing to stop it from building.

I could have curled my lips up into a smirk. Made a witty remark. Told her how hot she looked from this angle. But that would make a mockery of our friendship—and we were friends, even if she didn't know it yet. Hell, sometimes it was even hard to admit our friendship to myself.

She opened her mouth, and I braced myself for her words. "Pick yourself up, Damsel." My eyes hardened at the nickname, the context striking me harder than I would ever let on. I opened my mouth to retaliate, but she beat me to it. "Angelo De Luca is weak, and when you dwell on the punishment he dishes, so are you." She brushed the hair out of her eyes, giving me half a second to absorb her words. "But that's not who you are. Is it, *Day*?"

One day, when I didn't have my head so far up my ass, I would look back at this moment and realize it was precisely the moment I fell for Knight.

SEVENTEEN

> After all, damn it, what does being in love mean if you can't trust a person.
>
> — EVELYN WAUGH

RENATA VITALI

Girl power. Noun. Power exercised by girls, specifically in the context of supporting oneself and fellow women. Origin: coined by American punk band Bikini Kill. Alternative spelling: grrrl power.

Antonym: Laura Willis.

Laura had supporting herself down to a T. I would give her that. But when it came to empowering other women, she fell as flat as a slashed tire. It had taken me five seconds at Devils Ridge High to realize exactly the type of obstacle she would pose for me, and months later, I could confirm the accuracy of my initial assessment.

Which was probably why pickpocketing her phone wasn't the best idea I had ever had, but other than my nightly forays with Damian in his home library, boredom had become a sibling of mine. Plus, I needed a phone to contact Maman.

Devils Ridge, like other small towns, possessed more gossip than a lifetime subscription of *Us Weekly* magazines. Only, nearly everyone in this town had mafia ties, turning it into an incestuous community of shared dirty little secrets.

One of which was the ban that had been placed on phones for me.

My teachers kept me away from tablets, phones, and laptops. No one would lend me anything, Angelo had cleared the household of stray electronics, and I'd never ask Damian for a phone because I didn't want to break the tentative truce he and I shared by reminding him of how we'd met in the first place.

I wasn't normally a thief, though I happened to be good at it. The thin metal felt powerful in my hands as I leaned into my locker and typed out the password I'd seen Laura entering during AP English Lit the week before. It opened without trouble, and I pulled up her browser app and checked my emails.

None from Maman.

My head and hands buried in my locker, I drafted an email to my mom.

From: Renata Vitali
To: Margot Vitali
Subject: Earth to Maman?!

Hey Maman,

I tried to reach you months ago on a phone. It wasn't mine, and I no longer have access to it. I haven't heard from you, and

I'm worried about you. Are you okay? I'm sure Papà told you where I am and gave you orders not to contact me, but just know I'll be looking out for word from you just in case.

I'm staying with Angelo De Luca—he has a son!—at their mansion. Papà gave the order to remove communication privileges from me. Papà wants to silence me, Maman, because I saw him doing something he wouldn't want you to know. Honestly, I would rather tell you what happened in person. I know you cannot defy Papà and move me back to Connecticut, but maybe you can visit. I can tell you in person.

I miss you Maman. You're probably worried about me, but don't be. I'm fine. I'll stay fine, too. I just needed to tell you that I'm safe, and I need to talk to you. I'll find a way to get access to the internet again soon.

Love You,
Ta petite guerrière

A hand gripped my scalp and yanked my hair back before I could press send. The phone clattered to the floor as my face left the locker. Laura's eyes met mine. Crazed. So crazed I knew she'd forgotten her place below me in the mafia hierarchy. The hierarchy that was probably the only reason these kids had left me alone all these months.

Damian emerged through the crowd, his eyes leaping from Laura to me. We'd been doing the secrecy thing, and this marked the first time he'd been near me at school. There was nothing to out. We weren't in a relationship, but there would be implications to the complicated relationship we did have.

Still, I wondered what he'd say or do, so I waited for his reaction instead of sending an elbow backward into Laura's gut and taking care of this in my least preferred method of dealing with people—physical fights.

"Stop." Damian's voice bounced off the narrow hallway walls.

I liked where this was going.

He took a step forward, looking particularly menacing with the shiner Angelo had given him a couple days ago. "She's a Vitali." He shook his head when Laura's hand tightened on my hair—she had a thing for him, and his defense of me had to be eating away at her ego. "Stop, Willis."

My scalp burned, but it was worth it to see Damian defend me. I knew how he behaved at school by heart. He didn't defend anyone. He kept to his corner and let the kids come to him, like a king, indulging his loyal subjects. This… this was everything.

Laura turned up her chin, but it wobbled, and her hands shook on my scalp before she lowered her head in submission. "Because you're protecting her?"

"No." Damian's eyes flicked to me, and they speared me for all of point one seconds before he dismissed me with his gaze. "Because she's nothing."

And that was my cue to leave.

I swallowed my emotions, pushed my heel down onto Laura's foot, swung an elbow backward into her stomach, and twisted away when she released my hair with a surprised yelp. Violence didn't satisfy me, but I needed to get out of the hallway, and it was the quickest way. Plus, the De Lucas had invaded Devils Ridge. The staff would do nothing, and either way, in the eyes of the international syndicate court, my Vitali name justified any action I chose to take. I could kill Laura, and there would be no repercussions.

I didn't bother addressing either of them as I closed my locker door, swung my book bag over my shoulder, and made my way to the library for the rest of the lunch period. About ten minutes before the bell was set to ring, Damian pulled out the chair across from the table I sat at, a worn copy of *Nightmare Abbey* open before me. I'd just gotten to the part where Marionetta torments Scythrop. Fitting if you asked me.

"I never took you as an anti-romance type of girl."

I turned the page. "Was it my lack of faith in humanity that persuaded you otherwise?"

Our banter marked familiar territory, which he didn't deserve. He'd hurt my feelings, which meant I cared, and I *couldn't* care. His opinions shouldn't have mattered to me. They were only words, and he was a pitstop, not the finish line. He hated me; I hated him. That was the familiar territory that should have superseded this weird friendship that had burgeoned between us.

"You're mad at me."

Did it matter? This arrangement would be over when I turned eighteen in a few weeks and could flee without legal repercussions.

"Anger would require emotions, and I don't have any of those where you are concerned." I cocked a brow and met his eyes.

They were so talented at guarding things. At school, he played off his dad's onslaught of abuse well. But I saw the real him. The rage simmered on a loop, and I knew I would never figure out how to extinguish the flame. A part of me wanted to watch him self-destruct, just so I could be the one to pick up the pieces.

Some knight I was.

"Okay, I deserved that, but in my defense—"

"Those words are usually the predecessor to some lackluster excuse—almost always offensive, and one hundred percent likely to piss me off. You're better off stopping now."

He closed his eyes and ran a hand over his face. "I was an asshole out there, but it's better that way."

"Excuse me?"

"It'll get worse if they know we're friends. Plus, you can handle a few schoolyard bullies. I have no doubt about that, though I do doubt they can handle you."

My lips twitched, and I knew we were both thinking about the elbow I had swung at Laura. Violence was never funny, but I couldn't help myself. Damian's excuse could have been as simple as a De Luca protecting one of his own. I could understand that and part ways without spending more than a few sleepless nights dwelling over it.

But here he was, in front of me, and *that* I didn't understand.

"Why are you here, Damsel?"

"You have until the bell rings." He slid something across the table to me.

I glanced down at it.

A phone.

The library had been empty when I entered, but I still checked before clutching onto the contraband device. My mouth opened and hung there, unsure of what to say in this situation. Did I thank him for the phone or toss it back at him, offended at the idea that he could buy my forgiveness?

I didn't want to do either, so instead, I unlocked the phone, pulled up my email account, and sent the email I had drafted earlier before logging out and deleting the history. We had five minutes left until the bell rung, and I didn't know where this left us.

It wasn't like I thought we'd figure things out in five minutes, but not trying didn't feel like an option. I'd meant it when I likened us to kindred souls, chasing away loneliness in each other. I didn't want to lose that.

I only had a few weeks to go before I was old enough to leave Devils Ridge on my own. Damian shouldn't have mattered, but he did.

"Princess?"

Oh. I'd been staring. I slid the phone to him.

He stood and pocketed the phone. "See you tonight."

"Tonight?"

"Yeah. Tonight." He slid the chair back under the table. "This doesn't count as our library date."

Date, he'd called it.

Shut up, stupid pitter-pattering heart.

EIGHTEEN

> “It is not a shame to be deceived;
> but it is to stay in the deception.
>
> — OLIVIA

RENATA VITALI

The beige leather of Damian’s Range Rover caressed my skin. Probably the only smooth thing about this car ride. My chipped nails fiddled with a stray white hair on my hoodie. Short. Coarse. Dog fur, maybe, except I obviously didn’t have a dog.

My eyes veered to the driver’s side. Damian’s hand rested on the steering wheel, his body posture casual. If it weren’t for his black eye and my frumpy attire, we’d look like a million-dollar car commercial.

I’d gotten used to his black eye. It even faded a bit. The girls in school gossiped about it. They talked in the halls about how much hotter it made him. The guys fist-bumped Damian's shoulder whenever he passed, giving him props for the black eye as if the memory of how he'd gotten it didn't still haunt me.

I didn't know how people outside of school reacted, but judging by the horrified stares Damian received from the staff and faculty at Devils Ridge High, the De Luca members didn't like the idea of Angelo beating their golden boy. It didn't help that Damian did nothing to dispel the rumor that his father had hit him.

Once again, I examined the black eye, tried to stop the pure hatred for Angelo from consuming me, and had to confront the idea that I cared for Damian more than I'd like to admit.

"You're staring at me again."

I redirected my gaze, flicked the strand of dog fur from my hoodie, and stared out of the windshield. "Are you sure your dad's driver can't drive me to and from school?"

"The man's appendix burst, Princess. What do you expect from him?"

"What's the recovery time for an appendectomy again?" I could last a few days. It wasn't the end of the world.

"A week at the very least." His eyes cut to me.

"Keep your eyes on the road. This is precisely why Orlando should be driving me." Definitely not because I couldn't handle being this close to Damian.

He reached forward and turned up the air conditioner, his fingers so close to my body. "Orlando has one to three weeks of recovery left, and no amount of complaining from you will change that." The flat voice he spoke in did little to appease me.

I shook my head, my denial weak at best. "I'm not complaining. I don't complain."

He braked at a stop light and returned his attention to me. "Do you have a problem with me being your ride to school?"

I paused. "Did you say three weeks?"

"Yes." His fingers tapped the steering wheel, and he repeated, "Do you have a problem with me being your ride to school?" His probing gaze scorched my skin.

The stop light refused to turn green.

Come on, come one, come on.

Devils Ridge had to be the worst place for me to realize I had a heart. Small town. No way out. Unhinged mafia boss. The hottest guy I'd ever met everywhere I turned. And now we'd be stuck in a car together every morning and afternoon? No way.

My teeth dug into my lower lip before I opened my mouth again. "What happened to us not being seen together?"

"Everyone in town knows Orlando is in the hospital. They'll understand when they see you with me."

"Did your dad put you up to this?"

He slammed on the brakes and stuck his arm in front of me to stop my body from shooting forward. His head swung to me, and his eyes scraped their way up and down my face. "Are you serious?"

I looked down at where his arm touched my chest. "Yes."

No.

I didn't know.

Damian shook his head. "Angelo wanted you home, and you've seen how he's been hiding out all week."

I caught the implication. Damian had made the decision to drive me to school, rather than leave me with Angelo. Considering his motives meant considering the possibility that he worried about me, which would imply he cared.

Maybe one day, I'd be able to accept that without a fight, but until then, I'd keep my guard up and trust no one with my heart.

But it was getting harder and harder to temper my feelings.

NINETEEN

> Love cannot live where there is no trust.
>
> — EDITH HAMILTON

DAMIANO DE LUCA

The edges of my black eye faded by prom night, but the damage had been done. The regulars at The Landing Strip saw the ugly bruise, and they talked. Meanwhile, the girls helped plant seeds of doubt about Angelo's sanity.

Coupled with the fact that he was increasingly prone to violent outbursts, even in public, word spread. Angelo had gone insane. Gone was the quiet, reserved man who ruled back when my mom lived. The De Luca curse had seized him, people whispered. Yes, my black eye had confirmed.

See, syndicates always embodied loyalty, honor, and family. Angelo had already been chipping away at these values, and rumors of him beating me pushed them over the edge. They reached a new high.

I knew Angelo knew this, because he'd been lurking around the household, eyeing me up every time he could. He stopped visiting me at night a few days ago. He stopped leaving the house a few days before that.

Which was how I knew my next task would bring him over the edge. The last push before all the dominoes fell. It was less of a task and more of a list filled with bank account info and routing numbers. The De Luca coffers.

You know what to do.

And I did.

Whether it's the United States government, the Girl Scouts of America, Pee Wee football, or the De Luca syndicate, organizations only exist when money funds them. So, the day of prom, I drained the accounts.

Cris transferred the funds to new accounts we had set up last week when I brought him into the fold of my coup. The offshore accounts with the rerouted money belonged to holding companies I'd registered under Angelo's name.

Thanks to offshore privacy laws, I was able to transfer the money from the offshore accounts to new accounts with no one knowing. For all they knew, Angelo still had the money in his dummy accounts.

Cris tucked the computer we bought for this away in his backpack. "I'll have the laptop destroyed just in case they decide to track the IP address. I logged on through Angelo's private WiFi network, so it'll trace back to him if someone decides to go looking."

I slid a tie around my neck. "Tomorrow, payroll will come, and our accountants will realize everything's wiped clean. If someone looks, it will be traced to Angelo. If no one looks, either way, people won't get paid. Those who aren't already questioning will have his head."

"What will you do?" He watched as I finished adjusting the tie.

"Dude, are you going to prom? We just wiped nearly a billion dollars. I kinda want to go to Vegas and hit a high roller's table."

"First, Vegas is Rossi territory. They don't like us."

"No one likes us."

"I'll change that." I slid my feet into my Testonis and turned to face Cris. "Second, that money is not for us."

"I know. It's to rebuild the syndicate once Angelo is gone. Yeah, yeah, yeah."

People would lose money, turn against Angelo, and rally with me when I tell them I can use my home access to get the money back from Angelo.

Bye, bye, Angelo.

"Third, yes, I'm going to prom, and you should, too. We'll both need to act like nothing is out of the ordinary. I had an extra suit dry-cleaned for you."

Cris was adjusting his tie when he finally asked the question I'd been waiting for him to ask. "How'd you get the banking info? That shit's locked tighter than the Pentagon."

"If we get through this, I'll tell you."

TWENTY

> “Trust thyself;
> every heart vibrates to that iron string.
>
> — RALPH WALDO EMERSON

RENATA VITALI

Normal.

Two syllables. Adjective. Conforming to a standard.

Synonyms: usual, typical, or expected.

Antonym: my life.

Turning eighteen felt like it should have been a rite of passage. I didn’t feel any more or less like an adult than I had at seventeen. I didn’t celebrate my newfound adulthood with parties or friends. Heck, I’d forgotten it was my birthday until I woke up the next morning and Angelo De Luca told me eighteen was a little too old for his taste.

Maybe that was why I showed up to prom.

I wanted to feel normal, but in a town of mafiosos and their children, normalcy evaded me. Prom represented my last chance at normal high school memories. The crowded gym and paper decor screamed, "Normal!" The taffeta dresses and matching ties? Normal. Sitting at an empty table, watching other kids enjoy their senior prom? All too normal.

So, why wasn't I happy?

Maybe I didn't know what I wanted.

I certainly no longer wanted to be here.

I stood and headed for the hallway, grabbing a water bottle from the refreshment table on the way out. The library entrance nestled at the end of the hall welcomed me. I left the door open, so the hallway light could stream into the library, and took a seat on the floor.

I downed the water and spun the empty bottle, bored out of my mind but too stubborn to leave the only high school event I'd ever been to.

"You're the life of the party."

"No self-respecting woman should wish or work for the success of a party who ignores her sex. Susan B. Anthony."

"Not the kind of party I was referring to." He stepped closer until his feet were in my line of sight, next to the bottle.

I trailed my eyes up his body, taking in the three-piece suit he wore like he posed in a *GQ* feature. "No shit."

"So, you're in a grumpy mood, I see." He took a seat next to me and leaned against the bookshelf behind us. "What is it about libraries?"

"Nothing is less lonely than a room full of books." I breathed in. "And the smell. Definitely the smell."

He reached beside him and grabbed a random book, flipping through it quicker than he could possibly read. "Why are you here?"

"Why are *you* here?"

"Really?"

"Do you ever feel like the only real people in this world are the ones in these books?"

"Or maybe the world we're living in is a book, and we're just characters."

I rested my head against the bookcase and closed my eyes. "If that's the case, someone is reading me, becoming me, understanding me, and maybe I'm not so lonely after all."

He paused a beat, and the silence burrowed between us. "I'm sorry you feel lonely."

This was getting too real.

"Why are you here, Damsel?" I nodded in the direction of the gym. "You should be out there with your loyal subjects."

The lopsided grin he gave me shocked my system, and the calmness I'd always prided myself on fled. "Don't you mean *your* loyal subjects, Princess? You're the Vitali."

"I'm the Knight, and don't change the subject. Why are you here?" I leaned forward, and I didn't even consider why I held my breath as I waited for his answer.

"Let's dance."

"What?" I shook my head. "If we go out there together, we'll break their little minds." As far as I knew, no one knew about our friendship.

"So, we'll dance in here." I opened my mouth, but he cut me off. "Don't think too hard. If you want to dance with me, dance with me. As simple as that." He stood and turned to face me.

The second my palm pressed against his, I knew I'd made the right decision. A slow song drifted into the library, faint but enough for us to find a rhythm. My fingers gripped his shoulders as his hands slid around my waist.

I forced myself to keep breathing when he stepped forward, and my chest brushed against him. The first step we took was effortless. In sync without trying.

I rested my chin on his shoulder, and my nose brushed against his neck. I felt his Adam's apple bob against my cheek. "Thank you."

He didn't say anything for a moment, and the territory we drifted into felt dangerous. Risky. Like it could either be the best decision or the worst decision I'd ever made. I was almost thankful when he said, "Don't think too much of it," instead of something that would tip us past the breaking point.

Maybe he saw the million questions running through my head, because he dipped me and spoke into my ear. "Tell that brain of yours to shut up and let us dance."

"Why?"

He pulled me back up, and his grip on my waist tightened. "Because you'll find out."

That he cared about me.

"I already have."

His eyes darkened as they scanned my face. We'd stopped dancing after the dip, but he still held me, and I still clutched onto his shoulders.

My pulse was erratic.

Damn it, Heart.

My throat closed up.

Not you, too, Throat.

My knees buckled.

I give up, Body.

I kissed him.

Our lips pressed together, and instinct latched onto me as I explored his mouth. His tongue traced my lips. I parted them, and he slipped inside. His tongue stroked the roof of my mouth, and he took a step into me, backing me into the bookcase behind me.

The musty scent of books, and characters, and worlds mixed with his scent of bergamot and blackcurrant. I needed him closer, but I didn't know how to ask. My hands slid down his shoulders and pulled at the tucked edges of his dress shirt underneath his vest. I dipped my fingers under the shirt and explored the hard edges of his stomach muscles.

His mouth drifted from my lips to my jaw and down my neck. I cried out when his tongue traced my collarbone, then bit down. My right hand wrapped around his body and squeezed his butt cheek, but the phone in his pocket blocked my movement.

As if someone had dumped a bucket of water on my head, I lurched out of the lust fog. What had I done? We were… I didn't know what we were. Natural born enemies? Accidental friends? Neither felt right.

Maman hadn't contacted me yet, but I knew she would. I'd been eighteen for a week now. When she contacted me, I could leave. Damian only complicated things. He must have felt my waning enthusiasm because he backed up, giving me space.

My heart warred between feeling grateful and wounded.

It's not the first time he's hurt you, Heart. Remember when you first came here?

My heart wasn't having any of my logic.

He may have hurt me, but he heals so much better.

Damian's brows furrowed. "Knight?"

Panic lodged itself in my throat, and I forced some words out. Any words. "This means nothing."

Frustration flashed within his eyes. "Keep telling yourself that, Princess."

The lust fog may have eased, but I still felt heavy. Like layers of secrets and history weighed me down as I stood mere feet from the first boy I'd ever kissed. "I need air."

It took a moment, but he finally nodded. "I can take you home."

I agreed, grabbed the empty water bottle I'd chugged earlier, and forced myself to take steps toward the gym to get my coat from the coat check. A rivulet of sweat trailed down my cheek. I swiped at it with a hand that felt like lead.

My body swayed into Damian's as we entered the gym.

He caught me and steadied me just as he returned. "You okay?" When I nodded, his hand still on my elbow squeezed. "Stay here. I'll go get your coat."

I stumbled to the refreshments table a foot away, my dry mouth begging for a water bottle.

Laura met me at the table, a smirk pasted on her cherry-red lips.

"Still thirsty?" She looked at the empty bottle in my hand, then the row of water bottles with one missing. Mine.

It took me a moment too long to piece it together. That fog in my head pressed down with each second. She'd put something in the water bottles, water bottles only I drank from. Everyone was in on it.

Was Damian?

I shook my head and swayed again.

Like earlier, Damian caught me. "Ren?" When I didn't answer, he turned to Laura, his arms still around me. "Laura? Care to explain?" The hardness in his tone eased my worries.

He didn't know.

I let myself check out as they talked.

Laura crossed her arms. "I-I…We were just having fun."

Damian's head brushed my cheek as he turned to look at the water bottles. "You drugged her? What if I'd drunk from a water bottle? Would you have drugged me?"

"One of us would have stopped you!"

"Are you insane? She's a Vitali, Laura. Her family could have us all wiped from existence!" The gym had quieted, and Damian's shouts rang across the gym as he addressed the entire student body. "Have you all gone fucking insane?! Why would any of you go through with this?!"

Silence.

"Someone better fucking answer me. Now!"

"Laura said it was your idea."

I didn't know who spoke up, but he sounded like a chipmunk. I'd never loved chipmunks, but I'd always loved animals. Why didn't I love chipmunks?

My knees buckled again, and Damian all but carried me now. "Your punishment will be given tomorrow, Laura." He raised his voice. "As for the rest of you, you're all fucking idiots."

I looked up at him. "I'm an idiot?"

He closed his eyes, sighed, and opened them again. "No. Now let's get you home." He bent down and carried me bridal style.

My head lolled back. "I feel like a princess."

"You are a princess."

"But I'm a Knight. I do the saving, not you."

"Consider me a fellow knight. We're in a battle together. I'm doing what any knight would do and helping a fellow knight."

"Damian?"

"Yes?"

"I don't know what we're talking about."

His lips turned upward before abruptly shifting downward. "Rest, Knight. We'll be home soon."

The driver opened the door. Damian slid us into the car, and I closed my eyes as I sat on his lap, my head resting on his shoulder. When I opened them again, I was on my bed, and the room began to spin. Damian stood at the foot of the bed, an oversized shirt of his in one hand.

He followed me as I ran across the hall and heaved into the bathroom toilet. I took the shirt he offered, and he turned away as I changed out of my dress and into the shirt, which fell down to my thighs. It smelled like him. His scent eased the dizziness and caused tingles to spread across my flushed skin.

I blinked a few times until his face became clearer. "What's happening?"

"Laura gave you GHB." He helped me back to my room and onto my bed.

"What does that mean?"

"It means you'll be drowsy, dizzy, nauseous, sweaty, and tired. But you'll be okay." He hesitated as he tucked me into bed and pressed a kiss to my forehead. "You probably won't remember a thing."

I remembered that we weren't friends. "Why are you helping me?"

His jaw ticked, and he swung his gaze to the side for a moment. "Earlier, you said the only real people in this world are the ones in books. But you're real, too, and when I'm around you, you make me real. You make me alive." He took my hand. "It's the only time I don't feel like I'm just going through the motions."

A lopsided smile grew on my face. "I think I like you."

"I think I more than like you. If things weren't so complicated, I could see myself with you forever."

"Like when a princess and prince marry and live happily ever after?" I yawned and closed my eyes.

"Yes. Just like that."

"I'd need a ring." I snuggled deeper into the covers. "The princess always has a ring when she lives happily ever after."

Some shuffling interrupted my near slumber, and when a hand touched mine, I opened my eyes. The edges of my vision blurred, but I could see Damian crystal clear.

With the Sharpie in his hand, he drew a ring around my wedding ring finger. "And we lived happily ever after." He popped the cap closed, blew cold air onto my finger, then kissed the top of it. "Sweet dreams, Princess."

When I woke up, a thin black line drawn across my finger caught my eyes. I didn't know how it got there, but it felt important.

TWENTY-ONE

> Trust starts with a truth and ends with a truth.
>
> — SANTOSH KALWAR

RENATA VITALI

The seat pulled out across from me, and I swung my gaze up to Damian. We studied each other. He quirked a brow up, daring me to tell him not to sit.

I rolled my eyes. "Go ahead."

Two freshmen giggled as they passed our table in the corner of the school library. Usually, I ate near the center bookshelves during lunch period, but I couldn't sit there without flushing at the memory of Damian kissing me against them.

"We're in public," I pointed out.

"Way to go, Nancy Drew."

"What happened to not being able to be near me in public?"

"I think that no longer applies after I very publicly stood up for you at prom and we left together."

Yeah. That.

I scratched at my shoulder, stared at anything but him, before finally giving him the attention he deserved. "Thank you."

"What's that?"

"Thank you," I repeated louder, and what did you know? It didn't kill me. "Why'd you do it?"

His eyes flicked up and down my face. "What do you remember about last night?"

"I remember..." I cleared my throat. "I remember the library."

"That's it?"

Gosh, he was going to make me say it.

"I remember the kiss. I remember the gym. You took down Laura and everyone else. Then, you drove me home."

"And then?"

"And then, it gets fuzzy. You helped me to bed, and—" It occurred to me that he hadn't answered my question. "Are you going to tell you why you helped me?"

Why you kissed me...

"You don't remember what we talked about?" He looked like he wanted to say more, but he chose not to.

My brows dipped together. He was acting weird, not his typical, put-together self. His behavior made me antsy. I traced the marker ring around my finger, a nervous tick I'd developed over the duration of this conversation. I didn't even know where it had come from, but I drew comfort from it.

Damian's eyes dipped down and studied my movements. "What's with the ring?"

"I..." I faltered for something to say. Truthfully, I went to wash it off, but I couldn't bring myself to. It defied logic. "The marker wouldn't wash off."

He must have liked that answer because his toned changed. Brighter than it'd been. "It's marker, not a tattoo."

I changed the subject. "You haven't answered my question. Why did you help me last night?"

His eyes flicked to my ring again and lingered. "I helped you because this is happening, Renata. When we walk out the doors of this library, it'll be together. I've been working towards a goal for the past few years, and I achieved it prom night. I should have been happy, but I wasn't because I need *you*. You've given me a piece of myself I didn't even know was missing."

The bell rung, and neither of us moved.

Damian pulled his chair back, stood, and reached out a hand. "I'm going to leave right now, and if you leave with me, I'll know I've given you a piece of yourself, too."

This was Damian—the most guarded man I knew—putting himself out there. If I were being honest, his feelings mirrored mine.

I stared at his outstretched hand.

And then, I took it.

TWENTY-TWO

> Deception is one of the quickest ways to gain little things and lose big things.
>
> — THOMAS SOWELL

RENATA VITALI

Post-prom bliss.

It was a real thing. Not just something made up in movies. I knew this, because I felt it. Was I angry about Laura? Furious. But prom was my first real high school memory, and I wanted to cherish the things I remembered about that night. Like dancing in the library with Damian and my first kiss.

We'd shifted that night. Our nightly library dates turned into heated make-out sessions until the sun started to rise. We'd spend lunch at school in the library, reading beside one another and stealing kisses, because not a damn teacher or librarian would dare say anything to me or Damian. And we drove his Range Rover instead of being chauffeured, so we could spend car rides to school alone together.

We didn't put labels on our relationship, but the school year had already ended; as an adult, I could leave without legal repercussions; and it occurred to me that, if Maman were to finally find a way to reach out to me, I didn't want to leave.

I grabbed my henna pen and touched up the line I had woken up with the day after prom. I'd been doing this regularly since, and I couldn't explain it. The henna didn't feel permanent enough, but the next step would be a tattoo.

How could I tattoo something I didn't remember to my body just because I felt an inexplicable connection to it?

Answer: I couldn't.

I slipped a ring over the henna to cover it up. Though it looked ridiculous, I added rings on all of my fingers because I didn't want to explain the henna.

Angelo cornered me when I left my bedroom to meet Damian in his room.

I eyed Damian's door, urging it to open, before flicking an unfazed glare at Angelo. "Yes?"

He rested a hip against the wall and leaned closer to me. "You and my son seem close lately."

"Hmm..." I examined my nails. "When I last dined with the Romano boss, he had more important things to deal with than who his son chose to spend time with." Snapping my gaze to him, I smiled. "When was the last time you were invited to dinner with the Romano boss?" I laughed. "... or any syndicate head?"

His beady eyes narrowed, and the way he towered over me could easily be construed as a threat. "Have you heard of my grandfather, Ludovico De Luca?"

Who hadn't?

Crazy ran in the De Luca family, and it started with a man who'd kill his own child. In a world where loyalty and honor knew no bounds, the De Luca family held no place. Damian's sanity was nothing short of a miracle.

I measured his unspoken threat. "I know infanticide gets you off, but if not for dignity, try to have some self-preservation in that witless skull of yours. When you run this family to the ground, the only person in this town capable of rebuilding it is in that room behind you."

"Don't test me, Vitali. Don't be stupid." He leaned into my face, and his rancid breath seeped into my nostrils. "You should fear me."

I laughed, harsh and in his face. "You're unworthy of my fear."

It was true. But when Angelo pushed past me, and my hand connected with Damian's doorknob, I froze as Angelo's crazed laughter sent chills through my body. The frequent threats. The back whipping. The unhinged behavior. I shook my head and cleared all the ugliness out of my mind.

Angelo wouldn't kill his own son if I stayed.

Would he?

TWENTY-THREE

> "You can tell so much about a person by the way they leave you.
>
> — REDVERSE BAILEY

DAMIANO DE LUCA

"Knight?" I waited a beat as Ren stared into space, her hand raised like she'd been about to open my door. "Princess?" Another beat. "Ren?"

She lifted her head and lowered her hand. "Oh. Sorry. I spaced out."

"Are you okay?"

"Yeah." She moved around me and into my room.

I peeked into the hallway, but it was empty, so I closed the door behind us. "I heard my dad talking to you. What was that about?"

"Nothing." She laughed as she laid on my bed and closed her eyes. "Has he always been a crazy rambler?"

I crawled onto the bed beside her and grabbed her hand. "For as long as I can remember."

That was an understatement.

She skimmed her eyes across the room while I toyed with the rings on her right hand. She'd been wearing a dozen or so rings for nearly a week now. It was weird, but she didn't exactly have the style of a runway model. One of my favorite quirks, actually.

"What's that?" She tipped her chin to the left.

A facedown picture frame sat on the nightstand beside us. I'd knocked it down as soon as I'd seen it. She took her hand from mine, leaned over, and stood the frame upright. Ludovico De Luca stared back at us. Creepy fucker.

I shrugged, and it shifted the mattress. "My dad put it there a few weeks ago, after prom. Probably to fuck with my head. Who knows why he does what he does?" But he'd be gone soon, and that'd be one less thing for us to worry about. I laughed and leaned over Ren, dwarfing her body as I moved the picture frame facedown again. "I know we're related, but Ludo was one ugly motherfucker."

She rested her head on the pillow beneath her and bit her lip. So hot, I felt a jolt straight to my cock. Still hovered above her, I reached a thumb up to part her lips until her teeth no longer dug into them. "What's up?"

"Let's have sex!" she blurted. Her face brightened. It was cute if not wildly out of character.

Then again, she'd been like this lately. She was wild and reckless and crazy and so damned unexpected, I had no idea how to handle her.

I arched a brow. "I didn't know talking about Ludo was such an aphrodisiac."

She tugged at the bottom of my shirt, her greedy hands eager and frantic in their movements. "Ludo? God, no. But your body is over mine, and you smell good, and you look like you do, and you talk like you do, and you act like you do, and I just want you." Her tipsy eyes sparkled, drunk with what looked like lust and felt like trouble.

I buried my nose in her neck and grinned against her skin. "You know, I used to think you were like a robot. No emotions. Just articulate words delivered with no expression. Look what I've turned you into."

"Shush." She closed her eyes.

My mouth trailed up her neck to her jawline, which I peppered with kisses. She tilted her head and met my lips. We'd done this over the last few weeks. School ended. Angelo became more and more unhinged. The De Luca syndicate was falling apart at the seams, and I waited for my father to fall. My only constant nowadays was Ren, and I could do this—be with her—all day.

I could feel it rising in my throat, like an invisible liquid spouting from deep within me. Drowning me. I knew it wasn't there. I knew it was in my head. But it, like the annoying pounding of my heart, was tangible when Ren was around. She was drowning me, and I didn't want to be saved.

I deepened our kiss. My tongue stroked the roof of her mouth. She bucked her hips against me, grinding along my erection. Her fingers raked through my hair and tugged. I groaned into her mouth, and she reached between us and slid a hand underneath my jogger sweats and Calvin Kleins.

My cock glided across her soft palm. She wrapped her hands around my erection, and I thrust into her fist. Fucking it. My tongue mimicked the movement of my cock in her mouth. Reaching a hand between us, I pinched her nipples through her bra, so hard they pebbled in an instant.

She cried out into my mouth, and I swallowed her ecstasy. Her hands tore at my shirt until it ripped off. She used her legs to push my sweats and boxers briefs halfway down my legs. So fucking eager.

I leaned back, pulled her pants and underwear off her in one quick movement, and leaned forward again to place an openmouthed kiss between her legs. She cried out when I slid two fingers inside her. She was so, so wet, it dripped down my fingers, and they entered her with ease.

I curled my fingers until her wetness coated them. I pulled them out, tore her shirt in two, and snapped her bra in half. Her bare breasts sprang out, bouncing as the bra snapped. So full and round, I wanted to sink my teeth in them.

Instead, I slid my fingers inside her again—so deep, she arched her back off the bed. I gathered her wetness, slid my fingers out, and spread it around her nipples. My mouth latched onto the pebbled bud, and I sucked off the wetness. Flicking my tongue against it, I bit down.

She jerked her hips forward, and her pussy glided against my erection. My cock slipped past her lips, the head of it entering her. She was so tight, she sucked me in. I wanted to thrust forward, hard and fast, but I stilled.

My eyes closed, and I grit out, "Condom. Nightstand."

She surprised me by shaking her head. "Can we…?"

"Are you on the pill?"

"IUD. And I'm clean."

I nodded and slid inside her without another word. The urge to move deep and fast gripped me, but I kept my movements slow and measured in case she was inexperienced. Hooking her leg around me, she pushed me forward until I sank completely into her.

That was all I needed to pick up the pace. Her arms rested beside her head as I moved in and out of her. I grabbed one of her hands, holding it as I pushed inside her as deep as I could. She was so tight. I wanted to come inside her, then take her all over again.

My free hand explored her body. Pinched her nipples. Rubbed slow circles around her clit. Squeezed her hips. Gripped her waist, and pushed her harder onto my cock. I reached between us, gathered her wetness from her clit, and dipped my thumb into her mouth, so she could taste for herself how good she tasted. I could do this all day long. I could live inside her.

She came with her lips wrapped around my thumb. Her moans nipped my skin and shot straight to my cock. I pulled my thumb out of her mouth and pressed a kiss to her lips as I flipped us, so she sat on top of me. Gripping her hips on both sides, I picked up the pace from slow lovemaking to downright fucking.

As I drove into her, faster and faster, angling for her G-spot, her walls clenched around me, and my climax followed. I came inside her, her walls gripping me tightly. My eyes closed for a moment, and I took the time to appreciate this moment.

My father was falling, I was rising, and I had the girl of my dreams with me. I felt her lean forward and press her forehead against mine. My eyes stayed shut, and I breathed her in. Vanilla. Strawberry. That goddamned shampoo of hers mixed with the heady scent of sex. I could breathe her in all day.

"Day, I lov—" She cut herself off, but I knew what she'd been about to say.

Hell, I felt it, too.

For the first time ever, I felt liberated enough to feel this way.

I cupped her face and waited until she opened her eyes and stared into mine. "I'm in love with you."

"We're young."

"I know what I want."

"Me?"

A smile tipped my lips. "Yes, you."

She shook my head. "We can't."

"Why not?"

"I'm a Vitali."

And I was a De Luca. Would that always haunt me? No. I would dethrone my father, and I would make De Luca a name to be proud of.

I sat up, lifting her with me. "Pretty soon, my father will no longer have a throne, and there will be nothing in our way."

"Promise?"

"Always."

This lust-filled fog dowsed me, but I knew what I felt. I loved her. I fucking loved her. "I'm lucky you're here." I closed my eyes and relaxed, my guard the furthest down it had ever been. "I'm lucky they intervened."

"What?" She widened the gap between us, and her brows pressed together. "Who intervened? I was sent here," she ground out. "By my father."

Oh, shit.

I sobered up quickly. The fog washed away like rain pouring down on a dirty car. Never once had I spilled about The Benefactor notes to anyone but Cris. Except now, and I didn't even know why or who sent her here.

Her eyes punished me, threatened consequences if I didn't tell her the truth. I took her in before relenting, because yes, I wanted her to trust me. "Your dad didn't send you here."

That was all I knew. That she was sent here for a reason and not by her dad. I was telling her the truth, and I needed her to trust me.

She shook her head, her face resolute. "Yes, he did. I was there when he told me I had to come here." She seemed furious. Absolutely pissed. While I understood that I'd broken her trust, I also understood that she loved me. There had to be something else bugging her.

"Knight—"

Her eyes darted to the side, focused on the nightstand, and returned to me. "Tell me everything you know."

"I can't."

I didn't know anything, and she didn't believe me. Trust took so long to build, yet it slipped away so quickly, I couldn't catch it.

Her throat bobbed. "You're a liar."

"Princess, ple—"

"You're just like the rest of your family. Just like your dad."

My eyes flashed before I reminded myself she was just angry. She didn't mean it. This would tide over.

I caressed Ren's face. "You're mad. That's oka—"

She pushed me until I laid flat on my back with her hovering on top. "And you betrayed me. Know this…" She raised her knee, so it pressed painfully against my cock, her chest pressed against mine and lips brushing against my ear as she spoke. "If ever I am gifted the opportunity to betray you, I'll take it. If life hands me the chance to destroy you, I will. Today. Tomorrow. Ten years from now. I will always want revenge. And you will never stop looking over your shoulder."

Then, she fled.

She left Devils Ridge.

She left me.

EPILOGUE

> "I could never hurt him enough
> to make his betrayal stop hurting.
> And it hurts, in every part of my body.
>
> — VERONICA ROTH, *INSURGENT*

DAMIANO DE LUCA

Five Years Later

"You don't smile. It's kind of creepy." Cris sends a clown smile my way to make his point. Gone is his laid back, surfer vibe, replaced by a bespoke suit, sharp haircut, and fifty-thousand-dollar Cartier watch.

When I took over the De Luca syndicate, I didn't just make him my advisor. I made him my under boss—my second-in-command—too. One of the best decisions I've ever made.

"Smiling is for children and clowns. Overrated."

He slides a document to my desk and takes a seat in the leather chair across from me. "Your old man's been checked into a nursing home. Kind of cruel, considering he's, like, late forties, and everyone else is on their deathbed."

"That's the point. Does he have a roommate?"

"The worst."

I figure this is worse than prison or death to Angelo. There's nothing he hates more than the elderly, visits from happy grandchildren, and living without luxury.

Check, check, and check.

"And the other thing I asked for?"

Cris averts his eyes and takes in the office, like he isn't in here all the damn time. "No."

"No?"

"No, they haven't found her. The girl's gone. Ghosted." He hesitates, and I know I won't like what he has to say. "Maybe you should stop trying to find her."

"Or maybe I should try harder."

When Ren left my room five years ago, I didn't think she'd leave Devils Ridge entirely. She dropped off the grid, like only a Vitali could get away with. No matter how hard I've tried to find her since, I haven't been able to.

"Some would construe this as creepy."

He's right, of course.

We both know it.

I have everything I've always said I wanted. Angelo has been dethroned. I've dumped him into a nursing home far before his time. I run the De Luca family, everyone is happy, and we've been thriving. The Benefactor has disappeared. No more cigars. No more messages. No more instructions.

Everything is good.

I should be happy.

But I'm not.

Because Ren's not here to enjoy it with me.

"I just—"

"You're my best friend, Damian. I'm the only person in the position to tell you this. Let her go. She left you. She left Devils Ridge. She left the mafia. She doesn't want this life, and that's her choice."

"There's more to it. There has to be."

She wouldn't have just left because I kept the fact that her dad hadn't sent her here a secret. It was a breach of trust, yes, but it shouldn't have been a relationship ender. Not for us.

"Remember when my dad was sent to jail, and you told me to let him go. That he's dead weight?"

"This isn't the same." I look to the side and stare at a picture frame on the wall. A quote.

When the wrong people leave your life,
the right things start happening.

Cris got me this when I took over the De Luca syndicate. I thought it referred to Angelo, but now I have to wonder if he meant it for Renata.

He follows my line of sight. "Isn't it, though? You're still transfixed on her, and you can't be happy until you let her go. So, please, just let her go, man. How long is it gonna take? Five more years? Fifty?"

Try never.

I trace the camel bone case on my desk, a relic of the past. "Your advice is noted."

He nods his head, stands, and leaves with a parting message. "Let her go."

And he's right.

I should.

RENATA VITALI

The bell rings, and my students file out, running past one another.

"Walk, don't run!" I shout out to them. No use. It's still chaos.

Sally, one of the other second grade teachers, pokes her head in the doorway. "Some of the teachers and I are headed out for drinks tonight. Would you like to go?"

I shake my head. "I'm headed for my mom's for the weekend."

"Are you sure? I don't think I've ever seen you out."

That's because I don't go out. I teach. Stay home. Grade papers. Read a book. Eat takeout. Take baths. Pop out a glass of wine. Go to bed. Wake up. Then, do it all again the next day.

I smile at her. It's forced, but I doubt she knows that. "Sorry, Sally. My mom's been begging for a girl's weekend."

"Well, you work too hard. You've worked here two years, and I haven't seen you take a break once. That's not healthy."

"I appreciate the concern, but I'll be fine."

Her eyes look uncertain. Maybe she sees past my bullshit, but she says nothing. The people in small town Connecticut keep to themselves. They're not the type to ask invasive questions or give me a hard time. That's good when you're trying to lay low.

The drive from Connecticut to my mom's is short. Her majordomo

Gaspard greets me with a smile and leads me to the library, where Maman sits at her chessboard. She's staring at the pieces when I take a seat across from her.

"Hello, darling."

"Hey, Maman. Did you—"

"Get your pictures? Yes, my love. You have a problem." She hands me an envelope, which I take without a word. "This is the last time."

"But—"

"No 'buts,' Renata. Either you move on or you go back, but you must choose or I will make the choice for you."

"Fine." If she won't help me, I can find a way to do it myself. "How have you been getting these pictures?" I slide the images out of the envelope and stare at them.

Classic surveillance photos.

I grab a close-up shot. Damian is stepping out of a car. He looks so angry at the world, and I wonder why no one else notices. It's almost enough to make me want to save him. Almost.

"I have a friend."

"In De Luca territory?"

"You can't ask about Vitali things. You gave up that right." Her patient smile does little to soothe me, especially because she can't even begin to understand why I left the mafia. "Either you're out of the mafia or you're not, Renata. I pulled a lot of strings to get you out."

My eyes shutter closed. I left because this world embodies everything I hate. The fractured childhood. Being alone all the time. Letting Angelo De Luca and his stupid picture of Ludovico De Luca run me out of Devils Ridge.

I open my eyes and meet her gaze. "And I thank you for that."

Any other Vitali wife wouldn't have the power, but Maman makes friends everywhere she goes. She's friends with the wives of every powerful Vitali man, and Papà is so afraid Maman will leave him that he'll listen to her—to an extent.

"Then, truly thank me for that by moving on. Do what's right for you, Renata. You can move on, look to the future, thrive in your teaching job. I know you love learning and education. You should be happy."

"I am."

I'm not.

She sees past my lies, her eyes so understanding. "You're not. That's okay. He's your first love, Renata. First loves will always be the one you compare everyone else to. They'll live in your heart every day, and no matter how much you think you've moved on, they'll always have that special piece of you. For you, it's every time you step into a library and remember the memories you two shared in them. It's whenever you hear Texas in the news, and you wonder what he's doing right now. It's a million little triggers. It's a million little things. And if it were just one thing, you could bury it. But you can't bury a million little things, Renata. There's only so much space in the world."

"How do you know this? How do you know that's how I feel?"

"If you don't feel that way, he was never your first love in the first place." She reaches across the table and squeezes my hand. "I love you, Renata. I want what's best for you. You either need to go back to him or move on. This in-between state isn't healthy."

We both lied to each other. How can we trust each other again? It's not like trust comes with a free refill. My biggest fear is going to Damian and being told he doesn't want me anymore. That fear seizes me up every time I think of flying to Texas and begging him to believe I'm not just another person who disappointed him.

Don't be weak.

You're a Vitali.

Vitalis don't feel fear.

I repeat Papà's mantra twice in my head before I tell Maman, "I can't go back to him."

She releases my hand. "Then, move on."

It's not that easy, I want to tell her, but I bite my tongue. I don't want to hear her replies. I don't want to confront her logic.

Instead, I gather the courage to tell Maman, "When I was in Devils Ridge, Damian said I was sent there."

I told her nearly everything that happened in Devils Ridge—falling in love with Damian, fending off Angelo, and faking a fight to flee after finding the picture of Ludovico De Luca in Damian's room. But I never went into the specifics of the fight. Too painful.

Her brows draw together. "You were. We've been over this. Your father sent you there. He forbade me from visiting or contacting you."

I shake my head. "But why did you listen?"

Her remorse slithers across the table and into my heart. Making Maman feel guilty is like finding a stray dog and leaving him in a ditch. You just don't do it.

She dips her head and eyes one of the chess pieces between us. "I thought if I listened, he'd cut your trip short and let you come home to me."—He didn't.—"One of many regrets of mine."

"But Damian mentioned I was sent there. He implied it wasn't by Papà. I—" I take in her eyes. They're on the verge of tears, and I know if I push, she'll cry. One of many reasons I've never pushed. I take in a deep breath, then expel as much of the past as I can. "I'm sorry I brought this up. I know it upsets you."

"Oh, baby." She stands, rounds the small table, kneels in front of me, and grabs both of my hands, making me feel like I'm a kid again. "I love you, Renata. I worry for you. You have to stop asking for Damiano De Luca. You have to let him go."

"I will," I lie, because I'd rather break Maman's trust than admit to her that there's no letting go.

Loving Damian is trench warfare. It's digging deep, then clawing your way out. But sometimes, you have to accept that there's no way out.

ACKNOWLEDGMENTS

Chloe, I miss you every day. I try to put this feeling—this gut-ripping, bereft existence—into words. I can't. There are no words. Every second is spent missing you. Every minute is spent wondering what we'd be doing, how happy we'd be if you were here. No matter the time that passes, I'll always miss you. I'll always love you.

Rose, Bauer—you two troublemakers. Thank you for keeping me company; for being two tail-wagging, sloppy kisses-giving, insanely adorable puppies; for loving me without conditions. I love you both back.

L, I guess you're cool. (;

Ava, you nut.

Leigh, thank you for your help with this one, for being my Momager, for being an anchor in such a crazy industry.

Desiree, I'm so grateful to you. You're a gem. A rare find. I can't even explain how much everything you've done for me means to me.

Jayvin, thank you for spending time with the dogs when I'm buried with work. Best brother ever!

Heather, you're always there for me. You give me a shoulder cry on, someone to talk to, relate to. You're an amazing person and an even better friend. I'm lucky to have you.

Sometimes, people come into your life and blindside you. That's you, Heidi. You are stunning inside and out, and every time I talk to you, I find myself stopping to think about how lucky I am to have you in my life. Thank you for taking the time to be my friend, for investing yourself in my career, for caring about me, for being there for me.

To my admins—Krista, Brittany, and Amanda. You three are gems. You keep me sane. You make me laugh. The fact that you're in my life is something I don't take lightly. I appreciate and love you guys.

Bloggers! Whether you're a traditional blogger, Facebook blogger, IG blogger, or occasional reviewer, you've taken the time to support my work. You keep my career alive. You make me feel special. I'll never be able to show you how thankful I am, but know you all have a special place in my heart.

And last but definitely not least, thank you readers. My fifth book.

FIVE! It's just so insane to me, and there's no one I should thank more than you, my reader. There's no being an author without you guys.

XOXO,

Parker S. Huntington is from Orange County, California, USA. She has a Bachelor's of Arts in Creative Writing from the University of California, Riverside and is currently pursuing a Master's in Liberal Arts in Creative Writing and Literature from Harvard University.

She was the proud mom of Chloe and has two puppies, Bauer and Rose. She also lives with her boyfriend of five years--a real life alpha male, book-boyfriend-worthy hunk of a man.

facebook.com/parkershuntington

twitter.com/authorPSH

amazon.com/author/parkershuntington

bookbub.com/profile/parker-s-huntington

Made in United States
Orlando, FL
04 June 2022

18498840R00087